BOB CUPP

The Edict

Courses designed by Bob Cupp—more than 140 all around the world—have hosted U.S. Opens, U.S. Amateurs, many other USGA and NCAA championships, and numerous events on the PGA, Champions, and European tours; they have also been featured many times on "best new" and "top 100" listings in *Golf Digest* and *Golf Magazine.* He lives with his family in Atlanta, Georgia.

The Edict

A NOVEL

BOB CUPP

VINTAGE BOOKS
A Division of Random House, Inc.
New York

FIRST VINTAGE BOOKS EDITION, JUNE 2008

The Library of Congress has cataloged the Knopf edition as follows:
Cupp, Bob.
The edict : a novel / Bob Cupp.—1st ed.
p. cm.
Includes bibliographical references.
1. St. Andrews (Scotland)—Fiction. 2. Golf stories. I. Title.
PS3603.U73E35 2007
813'.6—dc22
2006036724

Vintage ISBN: 978-0-307-38592-5

Book design by Robert C. Olsson

www.vintagebooks.com

Printed in the United States of America
10 9 8 7 6 5 4 3 2

To Pam, my lifetime proofer

FOREWORD

I have known Bob Cupp for more than thirty years but needed only a few days to realize there was something unique about him. I was just starting my golf-course design business when Bob came to work for me, and like most course designers he had an obvious artistic side. But in his case the term *artist* transcended the obvious that comes with the ability to draw lines, to put form to terra firma, to turn red clay and gray sand into brilliant green fairways. Bob was an artist in the truest sense. Not a Christmas would pass that he wouldn't give my wife, Barbara, and me some handmade gift, be it a sculpture or a painting or the gift of song. Yes, it was usually around the holidays when we discovered or were reminded that Bob was quite the musician.

With most artists, you can see something of their range from the very beginning. Bob's breadth of aesthetic understanding made him an instrumental part of our early design business and he is among the men I credit for creating the cornerstone to the success we enjoy today. He has since established his own name and fame, and the genius we were fortunate to see at work thirty years ago is now alive in the pages of *The Edict*.

The genesis of this story can perhaps be found early in Bob's life. He was with me during a very formative period in my competitive and design career, and there were many moments when I could tell he was deeply moved by all aspects of the game. Yet there were always equal measures of imagination and wit that partnered with this emotion, such as the time he put a sign over his desk after my 1986 Masters victory that read *Sale! Green Jackets, 40% Off*.

This is not to say that *The Edict* was born completely out of Bob's healthy and vivid imagination. Who is to say that the story he weaves is *not* how things might have been? True, there are a very few who think that the game could have been invented by the wealthy, who had nothing else to do. But it could be that the game emanated (and perhaps my perspective arises from my deep-rooted and passionate appreciation for St. Andrews, Scottish golf and links golf, in general) from shepherds who literally had *nothing* to do for long periods of time while their dogs herded the flock.

This book presents a colorful story based on that assumption and then ties it into historic Scotland, from before the birth of Christ to the day the edict was announced—a span of almost 1,800 years. There are obviously no records, and it is not Bob's intent to present an academic argument in textbook form. Instead, he uses words rather than brushes to paint a picture for all of us to see. If nothing else, his story is at once believable and therefore entertaining.

This book's most important achievement, at least in my mind, is that it brings to life an era in which the game was crude but real—real enough to have drawn the attention of Scotland's leadership, which was critical or jealous of constituents who were perhaps having too much fun at a time when conflict was a very real threat. This can be seen as further proof that the game was that of the poor, not the rich, because the king certainly didn't intend to convert the wealthy into archers. For certain, the ban was a clear indication that golf was a part of life.

For anyone who has ever stood over a putt, no matter if it was the Open Championship or a dollar Nassau, for bragging rights among buddies or simply some glorious victory in the mind, the way the ball rolls can be a truly mystical thing. And if you've ever stood where a flock has just grazed, your first thought would be to take care where you step, but the second might be that if you only had a ball and a putter . . .

Jack Nicklaus

PREFACE

An edict, according to the *Oxford Dictionary,* is "an order proclaimed by authority." Such was the case in Scotland in 1457, when it was a free and independent nation, thanks to the heroics of Robert I (the Bruce) and William Wallace more than a century before. The Scottish king, James II, was a Stewart, and he wrestled with a volatile body known as the Scottish Parliament. Edicts were handed down to this group, but not all the king's wishes were carried to law; similarly, Parliament's wishes were not always given royal approval. This was a two-way street, with neither side holding absolute authority.

Academically, golf began in 1457. Historians will methodically insert this fact in the grand scheme of the human story because it is when the word *golf* appeared in writing, in an edict announced as law on the sixth of March. But, as with many things academic, logic does not always prevail. The ban on golf was to force Scots to focus on archery in order to help defend their realm from the English. James's insistence that this edict become law certainly implies that not only were a few shepherds out on the links, hitting balls, but also butchers, bakers, candlestick makers, the provost mayor, and very likely some nobles.

My conclusion is that in 1457 the game was booming.

This book expands on that ruling and hints at preceding centuries in which the game had evolved. Granted, this is largely supposition, but there must have been a series of fairly monumental events for golf to have become subject to law. Human nature is the primary guideline here. Man's indomitable spirit provides enough fuel for even the meanest imagination to produce a story line.

More important, my postulation of the game's development before the events of 1457 results simply from an examination of the game itself. For whatever reason, those beginnings are magical to me and I feel the need to define how it might have been.

My long-held belief is that golf has succeeded for three primary reasons: first, its physical, sociological and perhaps psychological setting encouraged it; second, man has phenomenal inventive capacities; and third, boys play games.

During the restoration of America's first actual golf course, Oakhurst Links in West Virginia, my curiosity about the origins of the game became so intense that they began to come alive in my mind: crackling visions of shepherds and flocks and links and wind, endless generations in obscure far-flung times fixed on experiences of motion and emotion that somehow became attached to their lives. Through daily activities, they passed all this along to their successors, timeless sets of fathers and sons sharing a common ground. What threads bound them? How did the game persist? What sequence did it follow through history to land at our feet as the complex, globe-straddling, billion-dollar enterprise it is today?

The game is fairly simple, after all, with only a few elements: the natural field of play; the entrancing flight, bounce, and roll of the ball; the hole itself, far and away the most cranial of subjects; and, finally, the competitions. Golf clicked, and civilization sustained it. Its survival is amazing considering that the Scots endured weather, time, their enemies and, most of all, themselves. Also, considering golf's quirkiness, please bear in mind that the game emanated from a people who think that what comes out of a bagpipe is music.

That would include me, because I'm stirred by that sound and the bones of *my* ancestors lie scattered about the moors and mountains of that fascinating and beautiful place.

There was a time when everyone contended with the daunting task of mere existence, and my story goes back nearly that far. Domesticating animals and raising crops instead of simply gathering food were major accomplishments, and training dogs as allies was another immense step forward for civilization and a monumental leap for golf. Dogs gave the game-inventing shepherd his most precious commodity, copious amounts of free time; when not hunching up against the brutal weather or pulling a sheep out of a hole or a gorse bush, the shepherd kept busy enough, making useful things, finding food and the like, even hitting or rolling a stone or a proper ball. But through the efficiency of his dog, who learned to constantly circle the flock, he found himself freed from the relentless requirement of physically chasing animals. He also found himself alone, often for days.

The loneliness of the primordial linkslands, human ingenuity and insatiable human competitiveness were the foundations of golf. The game was born, essentially, out of boredom.

Most of us learn games growing up under the rule of the unelected dons of boyhood, following rules that civilization has refined and embraced. But the shepherds had no such models. They were the first, so the development of *their* games took longer. But at the end of the day, in our youth and for many of us into adulthood, we're just like them, constantly testing ourselves and others in battles of skills and wills, driven by some deep-rooted need to compete.

I have fond memories from the 1940s when my father read Keats or Dickens to my brother and me while we writhed on the floor at the foot of his big blue velvet chair. Every once in a while he read about Doubleday or Naismith, Ivy League football or Major Walter Clopton Wingfield's pansy—as I thought then—game of tennis. Hence I knew early on about people who'd *invented* games and I slid inevitably, if unconsciously, into empathy.

But the game that puzzled me the most—the one for which Dad's books never named an inventor, the one that took up the most space and didn't seem to have any real dimensions, the one I played a lot—was golf.

Golf just *was.*

Finally, it is obvious that no person or organization in this millennium is smart or powerful enough to change it. Golf is what it is. We're all hooked, and it seems unlikely to go away.

I wanted to tell this imagined tale before I get run over by a truck or something. It is neither academic nor official—but it's both logical and woven into the fabric of Scottish history. Perhaps I have stepped off the rim of the Grand Canyon onto a thin wire of historic facts, holding only a long pole of supposition for balance—but here goes.

The Edict

Surrounds

A SOLITARY FIGURE slumped in front of a mossy stone building in slowly drifting mist, the hood, sleeves and shoulders of his leather jerkin, leggings and boots heavy with moisture. A leather shoulder bag sat by his feet on the sodden path, its strap dangling loosely from his shaking hand. The long leather sheaf across his back masked an unstrung bow and an empty quiver.

The man, Trailin, stood motionless, burdened, his eyes moving from the gate to the ground to the peak of the crow-stepped gable searching in vain for relief. Morning light was emerging. His heart thumped in anticipation of a duty he knew would be the worst of his thirty-four years.

He glimpsed movement past the granite cornerstones at the side of the house, a heel and the hem of a cloak slipping quickly out of sight. Silence again, but within a minute another figure appeared in the mist, a great hulk of a man clad in leather and fur, with a massive beard and hair wild from sleep.

"Trailin Carrick?" he called.

Trailin's duty had arrived, and after a moment's silence he answered. "Aye, my lord."

More silence.

"And Daniel?" Calgacus said, slowly and softly. "Will he be comin' then?"

Trailin sagged. "Nae, my lord," he said haltingly, "he willna."

Calgacus's great head and beard lowered to his chest as he steadied himself against the great cornerstones. Trailin began to shiver.

"I'm so sorry, my lord. Promised to look after him but dinna bring him home; I couldna carry him. I put him there, where he served. Ye'd've been proud, my lord. He rode beside the Black Dooglas himself."

Trailin painted a picture for the old man, by which Calgacus could remember his youngest son; of the Shiltron, a body of men under large wooden shields protecting themselves from the rain of death from above, and holding long, heavy, brutal pikes braced against the ground, raised as the English knights attacked, skewering either knight or horse; and of Daniel charging nobly at the flanks of the clambering English armor.

"It was there he fell," whispered Trailin. "Thomas Patersone saw him go down too and once the schiltrons did their business, Thomas picked him up, runnin' to where I was tryin' to cross back over the river."

Calgacus listened quietly, dredging scenes from his own war-torn memories.

"I *saw* them comin', my lord, like an ugly dark cloud in the air. Couldna get to where they was layin'—arrows coverin' 'em both, not two hundred steps away."

"Patersone too, then?" Calgacus asked.

"Aye," Trailin whispered.

"Bastards! Damnable English longbows!" Each word was spat in vitriolic hatred. He pushed his weight from the wall and shuffled slowly forward.

Trailin could finally see his lord's rugged but trembling face. The old man was a relic, a tribal chieftain named for an ancient Pictish ancestor who faced the Romans more than a thousand years before. This Calgacus was now past sixty, no longer a commanding presence but still held in deep affection. Trailin Carrick was a freeman, an independent forester whose family supplied the village flesher with fresh game for barter or silver. He and Thomas Patersone, a common shepherd, had been conscripted for this war, but Daniel, Calgacus's last son, of eighteen years, had insisted on going, to establish himself, to become a man, to make his father proud. Though he would no longer grace the rolling countryside of Fife, young Daniel had succeeded on all three counts.

"I failed ye, my lord."

Calgacus placed a giant hand on Trailin's shoulder. "Nae, lad, ye dinna," he said, pushing slightly with each syllable. "Nae. Ye're an archer and had ye been guardin' him, he'd've never seen the flash of steel. He followed his heart and made me proud. It's over now," he said, letting out a great rush of breath, "though I'm grateful to ye for lookin' after him."

Trailin had no need to express his regret. Solemn contrition cloaked his weary body, sagging in exhaustion from the three-day walk to Fife from the headwaters of the Solway Firth in the land called Galloway to the west.

It was October 26, 1448, three days after the battle at the River Sark. Hugh Douglas, one of the legendary Black Douglases, the Earl of Ormond, had led the Scottish army to victory against the Earl of Northumberland, up from Carlisle. Over centuries of brutal clashes between Scotland and

England, one glaring Scottish failure had emerged time and time again, scattering the flower of their youth into the sand. For more than two hundred years, the Scots had never answered the English longbow with any degree of success. Their fortunes in this battle, though victorious, also carried the terrible agonies of the butcher's bill.

"Trailin, lad, what of Mary Patersone and the lad Caeril?"

"Aye, my lord. Ah, I must go there yet. Dimmin' business, this. Young Caeril is my son's best friend. Oh Lord, this will hurt. Caeril'll be growin' up fast now. Poor Mary."

"Dunna go just yet. I'll come with ye; it's my fault too. Patersone was a good man." He turned to the small group now standing at the corner of the house. "Groom!" he called out. "Two mounts, lad, and be quick!"

In a matter of minutes, one horse was led up the path from behind the house and another, hard on its tail, was being saddled en route. Once they were mounted Calgacus looked down, shuddered, then explained that Daniel had fallen in battle at the River Sark.

"Trailin and I are goin' to Mary Patersone," he added.

Now everyone knew that Thomas was also a victim. They stood, heads bowed, as the two horsemen made off down the lane at a canter, disappearing quickly in the cool swirling mist.

It was a solemn, silent procession, the creak of leather, the soft plop of hooves in the dirt and the occasional huffs from the horses falling muffled in the fog. In a short while the men faced a far more ordinary house, wattle and daub, with a sod roof and animal pens all around. Their movement was certainly detectable, and as Mary stirred a stew in the iron kettle hanging in the hearth, she stopped to listen, then looked out the half-open shutter. She recognized both of them. In that instant, her mundane daily activities became intense and then froze, and her heart seemed to stop. Immediately, she knew.

The wooden spoon went to the floor. She gathered her shawl and bolted through the door. Calgacus and Trailin had no time to say anything. She knew why they were there and Thomas was not.

"Well?" Mary demanded, her eyes fierce. "He's dead then?"

The two men, taken aback, dismounted, each with a troubled glance at the other.

"If he was just hurt, ye wouldna both be here now, would ye? Well?" She was shouting, though addressing her lord and a dear friend. "Say it, then, just say it!"

The men found no words.

"How?" she shouted.

The answer came in one word.

"Bow," Trailin said, as he crossed himself.

Mary froze and then shrieked as the grisly image materialized. The men began moving forward to console her, but she lashed out, screaming, waving her arms and shaking with rage, her hair flying—trying somehow to drive this vision from her mind. "Why? Why can't we learn! Why can't we *see*? How many of ours have gone down with English ash through their bodies, lying four or five deep in their own blood—in *our* blood? I know those stories, those awful tales of Spottsmuir, Halidon Hill and Neville's Cross, and to them we're addin' the River Sark now, are we? The Douglas—he's dead too, then?"

"Nae, Mary," Calgacus told her. "Douglas prevailed and drove the English back nearly to Carlisle. Chased 'em down, he did, and cut 'em up. Burned Alnwick and Warkworth."

Trailin and Calgacus, amazed at her recall of the carnage of battles in which only a handful of Scots out of thousands had escaped, tried to calm her, but in vain.

"So ye'll go on with yer lives then, leavin' me and Caeril here alone? Oh, poor Caeril. What'll we do? My lad has nae father. Ye'll just go on back home to yer own families then?"

Trailin was cutting his eyes over his shoulder, toward Calgacus, and she stopped, eyes widening.

"Nae!" she gasped, looking at Calgacus. "Oh, nae, my lord. Where's Daniel?"

Both men bowed their heads.

In the enormity of her baying agony, she collapsed into sobs. Both men moved to catch her, but Mary clung suddenly to Calgacus. This was nearly unheard of, a serf in the grieving comfort of a master, but it was no ordinary man who held her.

"Cry on, Mary," he whispered. "Cry for yer Thomas and cry out the hurt. A good man he was. Cry as long as ye must."

Mary finally raised her head and reached out to touch Trailin's arm. "Aye," she choked, "we've lost our men. Oh, Thomas! And Daniel, as beautiful a lad as ever rode the fields of Fife. Oh, my lord, I'm so sorry. Thank ye both for comin'. God bless their souls."

They were taking her inside when Micael, Trailin's son of ten, came up the path. His father turned to embrace him and mumbled, "Caeril's father and Daniel, both gone. Find Caeril. Bring him home and tell him to mind his mother."

"Just left him, Da," the boy said gravely. "What'll I *say*?"

"Dunno, son, but he needs to be here soon."

Micael turned away, but Calgacus's large hand turned him about to face him. The hulking old warrior's eyes narrowed as he said, through clenched teeth, "Tell him we're here, lad. Maybe that'll break it to him and ye won't have to say the words. Go, lad. Go fast."

Micael exploded onto the path. Life would go on.

. . . .

THE SCOTS, in spite of colossal losses, seemed doomed never to acknowledge the power of the longbow. However, and in the purest historical sense, this tragic oversight would rise to the fore just nine years later and become instrumental, strange as it may seem, to the story of golf. The game's time had come, but would collide with the Scots' dread of the longbow.

Giant slabs of pure subpolar air slide over the surface of the North Sea, unimpeded by land until they reach the crags of Fife. On the worst days the water is a green-tinged gray. On the blitzed horizon the sky turns to the color of ash, accentuated by whitecaps as far as the eye can see, precursor of a spectacular show at the break of land.

The sandstone substrate of the east coast of Scotland rises and falls from nearly a hundred feet above the waves to well below sea level, and over time this has determined the coastline. Where it is high, the land juts into the sea as rocky crags. Where it is low, we have golf. In spite of the constant hissing, whumping rhythm of the powerful waves against the blackened crags, the ledges resist. In the lows, the sea advances inland, hollowing out the bays. It is here, not on the rocky crags, that the sea deposits fine round particles of sand. This is also the terminus of inland surface flows, which transport fine sand deposits toward the sea in cascading creeks and gently flowing rivers, meeting the incoming waves and creating constantly replenished plains of sand. The wind then carves these loose particles into raucous landforms that are quickly covered by grasses, the immortal Agrostis, which formalizes the shapes. Fine-bladed fescues and bentgrasses proliferate in the cool moist air. Only the meanest of winds, raging seas or great floods can move the rows of dunes. Otherwise, the changes are slow and subtle. The dunes are scoured from the windward side and the airborne particles deposited leeward, causing the dunes to creep across the landscape, undetectable in the blink of a human lifetime. Everywhere these vast areas became known as links, the space that *links* the arable land with the sea or, more poetically, the sleep in the corner of earth's eye.

The sand here is too dry for crops, but aggressive grasses make the links into natural grazing lands. At various times of the year, wild roses, forget-me-nots, daisies, thyme, Scottish lovage and dove's-foot cranesbill blend with the fescues, bents, gorse and marram grass in a soft, solitary, timeless, pastoral blanket.

The links contain multiple shapes from a few inches high to a hundred feet or more. There are no trees but some dark green brush, spectacular against the tan grass. The most endearing but subtle characteristic for golf is that, given the absence of trees and the endless variation of shapes, there is no possible yardstick by which to judge distance accurately. The links are always deceptive. Also, if the uplands are out of sight, it is an easy place in which to become disoriented. A man with a club and a ball faces more raw excitement, more extemporaneous challenge, more subtle natural beauty and more perfect ferocity of weather here than on any other terrain in the entire world. The links scream for a flying or rolling ball. Surely golf would happen here before anywhere else on earth.

But why did the game not emerge in the desert, the plains of Gaul, the mountain meadows of the Alps or, indeed, anyplace that had flocks and shepherds? There are links in other parts of the world, grazed often by sheep. Golf did not begin there because one prime ingredient, one unarguable, incalculable element, was missing, the mighty Scot. They are a basic but complex, bucolic but ingenious, quiet but steely race. They should have been frustrated by the conditions, both natural and political, but it seems perhaps that the quotient of pure resolve in these persevering characters was, and is, monumental. The Scots were, in fact, very much like the links in which they subsisted: always subtly changing, occasionally ravaged by upheaval; but at the core the links are sand and the Scots are—well, Scots.

It is not likely anyone will determine precisely when sheep appeared in the linkslands. Perhaps they were there before man, but we know they were herded four thousand years before the birth of Christ on the island of Soay in the St. Kilda group. This hardy animal elevated man's existence through the ages, providing, as well as food, the yarn for various types of woven clothing and hence warmth, materials derived from nearly every part of the animal's body and the new craft of their keepers.

The Soay sheep are relics of prehistoric husbandry, but by the time the Romans arrived in Britain, their descendants had been bred to respond to dogs.

Sheep have thrived because they *need* man, and man was quick to recognize the benefits of the relationship. But sheep also provided a significant contribution to golf: they can graze turf to a spectacularly smooth playing surface. Sheep do a much better job of this than rabbits, and when they move on to greener sections, the patches in their wake make a perfect playing field—except for dung, of course, and just a sweep of the foot clears that away. Such clipped turf, natural yet organized, is the propitiation of civilization. There is simply something very comforting about it.

It would be on the high ledges by the sea where man would choose to live, near the grassy links on which to graze his stock and, ideally, a river. But even in those locations, particularly along the eastern coast of Fife, immense natural forces—surging seas, pounding rain and nearly incomprehensible wind—contributed to the resolve of the people living there. Such a place was south of the Eden River estuary and the great expanse of grassy links beside the plateau called Kirk Heugh, the Church Hill, just fifty feet above the gray fury of the North Sea. At this time, the small settlement was called Muckros, Headland of the Wild Boar, which became Kilrymount or Kinrymount (also Rigmund), Cell of the King's Mount.

So it was in such a place that humans in the sixth century set about constructing a shrine: the first Church of Saint Mary on the Rock, the rock being "The Lady Crag." But they were either devoid of any appreciation for nature's power or so overcome by religious fervor that they did not believe they could be denied. The believers were Culdees, a Celtic sect, which led a peaceful existence with their families, caring for others and praising their God as they'd been taught in their native Dalriada, or Ireland. Before long, though, owing to the brutal weather, there was no trace of the building. Sometime later, before the end of the millennium, they tried again, farther back from the edge of the cliff, but with similar results. Today, only the foundations of that structure remain.

There are two conflicting myths as to how Andrew's bones arrived in Scotland, one by land and the other by sea, and both are worthy of consideration. Andrew of Bethsaida, brother of Peter, both apostles of Jesus of Nazareth, had been brutally crucified in a tiny Greek coastal town of Patras on a saltire, an X-shaped wooden cross that is now the basis of Scotland's flag. Andrew's remains were acquired from Patras by Constantine, who then took them to Constantinople.

In the seaborne version, an unknown guardian of the relics, possibly Regulus, had a vision that he was to take them to a land that would be revealed to him, and was subsequently shipwrecked off the coast at Rigmund, came ashore and assumed this was God's providence.

At the same time, the Pictish king Ungus, then fighting for his life against invaders from the south, heard the voice of St. Andrew offering victory if Ungus would agree to devote a tenth of his wealth to the glory of God. News of a miraculous restoration of sight to a blind man soon led him to Regulus, and the king decided to name the place St. Andrews in honor of the bones. However, the historical record suggests that Regulus lived somewhere between 573 and 600, and Ungus between 731 and 761, in which case, obviously, they would never have met.

The more likely version took place in the eighth century. A missionary of the church of the Irish saint Columba who was named either Regulus or Riaghail, settled above the sea at Muckros and established that religious community which eventually gave way to the Culdees. Sometime later, between 732 and 761, Bishop Acca, a known collector of relics, was expelled by the pope from his seat at Hexham and fled north to the Pict communities in Fife, taking Andrew's remains. How he got the bones from Constantinople no one knows.

Ungus plays in this version as well and supposedly was sufficiently impressed to bestow Andrew's name on the place.

In either case, the people immediately set about preparing proper protection for their ecclesiastic treasure, and it would be Andrew who would become the patron saint of Scotland rather than Regulus (St. Rule) as the cult of homage and pilgrimage grew around the disciple's relics.

Somewhere between the ninth and eleventh centuries, a much larger structure than the simple stone building on the cliff was under way, this with a great stone tower that measured more than 130 feet to the peak of its wooden spire. It became the Church of St. Rule, named for Regulus. The majority of this structure's gables and walls, like the first two Culdee churches, toppled before the elements, but the tower of St. Rule remains to this day a masterpiece of masonry. Its hundred vertical feet of narrow steps is a climb through a millennium of history; from atop this grand edifice it is possible to take in the distant moors, all whispering of momentous events, bloodshed, courage, treachery and heroism.

By 1160, the wicked wind, as though driven by some demonic force, had demolished all or most of these three holy structures. But it has been said that those who refuse to acknowledge history are doomed to repeat it. That same year the Augustinian Bishop Arnold of St. Andrews, under the watchful eye of King Malcolm IV, began work on what would become the largest structure in Scotland and the third largest in all of Britain, a cathedral nearly 400 feet long and 170 feet wide at the transept with a center spire reaching a height that might have been in excess of 200 feet. The inside width of the nave, including the side aisles, was more than twenty paces.

As with all the grand cathedrals of the Middle Ages, its construction was a saga of multiple lifetimes, of evolving trades passed from father to son, of artisans, guilds, injury, death, discoveries, adjustments, diligence and exemplary dedication. Kings rose and fell, bishops were consecrated and died and, through it all, work continued that defies comprehension. Stones were hewn from the quarries, trimmed, hauled, hoisted and fitted, great stone by great, elegantly carved stone, each marked by its carver. Eventually, the Cathedral of St. Andrews emerged as Scotland's consummate statement. Bishop Arnold was followed by Bishops Richard, Roger, Malvoisin and Wishart, over almost 160 years, until Bishop William Lamberton finally stood at the gleaming tapestry-draped altar with legendary King Robert I, the Bruce, in 1318 and sent echoing chants of consecration into the massive rafters and off the glorious stained-glass windows.

A wicked fire took its toll in 1378, and in 1409, a full 250 years after it was begun, a blast of monumental wind sent the south gable of the transept crashing back into the building. But like their forebears, intrepid in their dedication, stolid in their determination, the Augustinians and the town built it back by 1430.

Along with the cathedral came the priory, projecting off the south transept away from the wind. This was the administrative center of the church, featuring a dormitory for the monks, a refectory where they took their meals, a chapter house in which they conducted official business, a wing known as the West Range that served a variety of purposes and a cloister that fostered meditation. With its grand yard, or close, and ancillary buildings, along with the now ancient St. Rule's Tower and the turreted Abbey Wall, the cathedral dominated the plateau, separating the town from its tiny harbor.

Nearby, on its own promontory into the bay, a classic castle was begun in 1200 by Bishop Roger, who evidently was more interested in this, his own residence, than in the cathedral, and it was completed much faster. A series of heroic assaults shuffled ownership back and forth between the Scots and the

English numerous times, each with varying degrees of destruction and reconstruction, sometimes burrowing through solid ledge rock to break inside in a surprise attack. Kings were born and educated there, and dignitaries stayed in royal opulence while prisoners rotted in the infamous "bottle dungeon," carved straight down into that same solid rock.

The relics of the gentle apostle were indeed a treasure, because St. Andrews soon became the destination of pilgrims from as far away as Europe.

FROM 1440 TO 1465, as luck would have it, the bishop of St. Andrews was the shining star of all who had gone before or would follow. James Kennedy was a wisp of a man with a bald head and a great eaglelike nose. He was of royal lineage, descended directly from none other than Robert the Bruce and a grandson of Robert III. But he chose celibacy and dedication, becoming a prelate of piety, honesty and sterling integrity. He lived simply, dressed sedately and reinvested the vast revenues of the church into the see and the city. He governed quietly and confidently for a quarter of a century until he died of natural causes. He founded St. Salvator's College in 1450, made provisions for the education of the poor and, as one of the Old Lords of Scotland, guided two kings through minority reigns following the untimely deaths of their fathers. In the history of Scotland, and in the story of golf, he looms large.

Nationalism had been running high for over a hundred years and—though poverty abounded in most of the realm—Fife was flourishing and so, at its heart, was St. Andrews. Fabulous structures, ecclesiastic headquarters, frequent royal visits, the booming fishing industry and far-reaching international trade caused King James II to refer to eastern Fife as the "golden fringe on a beggar's mantle." Trades and guilds were thriving, invention was rampant and a monetary system had been established; wealth and creature comforts were coming to people who in the past had had none. Formal burghs flourished, and society was beginning to form almost as we know it today.

Politically, the Scots had been battling the English for as long as anybody could remember. They retold legends about the Romans and had survived and even absorbed the brutal Vikings. Now a steely race that savored freedom as much as any nation ever, they were not about to give it up.

"For so long as a hundred of us remain alive, we will yield in no least way to English dominion. For we fight, not for glory nor for riches nor for honor, but only and alone for freedom, which no good man surrenders but with his life." This is a modernized excerpt from the Declaration of Arbroath, written by Scottish nobles to the pope in 1320, requesting that the church recognize Scotland as a nation.

As golf emerged, St. Andrews was an ecclesiastic cornerstone of the Scottish universe, a thing of wonder, the gleaming jewel of Christendom on the edge of howling gray-green waters by the soft rolling links.

The Game

IN THE MID-FIFTEENTH CENTURY, golf was part of this teeming and vibrant society. A small group of elite players from all walks throughout Scotland met in competitions that then gave birth to a hierarchy of nobles, professional people and clergy known as the United Golf Honours Society. Cottage industries manufactured clubs and balls, and there was a rudimentary form of golf design. None of this could have existed without a following of men and a few women who loved to see the ball arching into the sky, borrowing against the wind or bumbling along the unpredictable slopes of the earth; they appreciated masterful execution because their own attempts were woeful by comparison. Golf to most was just a fanciful outdoor exercise. To a very few, it was life. In this burgeoning era the game was a luxury—not the absurd decadence we associate with it today but a luxury in the sense of recognizing recreation as an important new element of daily life. Civilization was changing, and golf, the Scots' own concoction, was one of the benefits.

. . .

IN 1456, a partner on the links might have been a shepherd, a carpenter or the provost mayor; class lines, aside from nobility, seemed to evaporate. Almost everyone played, and golf was flourishing, building excitement and anticipating the future. The Scots cared dearly how well they individually played this game, filled with mirthful joys and tolerable miseries. Interestingly, a player's talent was second to how well he managed his achievements and difficulties. Golf exposes the soul for all to see, and those who didn't play at all were suspect. If old Donald foozled and then mistreated his clubman, his mean-spiritedness was confirmed. If Katherine paid more attention to her outfit than to her windcheater, she would be deemed vain. If *anyone* was observed improving his position, he would soon be regarded an untrustworthy dog. The entertainment value of golf was thick with hilarity and Scottish humor.

Common serfs who played well might be partnered with nobility or the rich, and big-stakes games could change lives. Golf became the truest portrait of each player's ultimate self, and the Scots seemed to love this about the game more than anything else.

In an era when war and death were seemingly imminent at every turn, whether in English invasions or in various quests for the crown from within, golf stood in remarkable contrast. For centuries it had been a solitary activity in primordial surroundings—a hedge against the boredom of shepherding—but now it had become a game for the mind or, more accurately, the spirit, with the potential to exist as long as the species that had invented it.

And so, in late winter, when there were few crops to tend

and space between the religious holidays, the Scots had time to determine the best player in the land in a competition that had as much to do with celebrating golf as finding a champion. There were a number of good players and a handful of great ones, and every year they battled through loosely conducted local and regional qualifiers. The site of the finals moved around some, but as the game grew and the fame of St. Andrews increased, the links by the bay and the great estuary gradually became *the* place.

The game had not yet escaped the traditions of its forebears. The shepherds merely *found* the holes; far from the fixed routes of today, they were in fact completely temporary, playing out from the flock and immediately back, no matter where the flock happened to be at the moment. (Interestingly, this made flocks of sheep the first clubhouses.) The holes floated about the links like clouds in the sky. The quality of the golf in any given place actually depended on the dunes, the plains, the kettles and kames, the density of turf and the fickleness or power of the wind. A good hole was one that provided momentary escape from boredom and appropriately tested the skills of various players. In essence, it was personal and totally fluid. Any complaint about conditions was anathema to the game itself.

The shepherds began playing toward or over some dangerous feature, just to make things exciting, and from there to the hole. The length of the hole was based on the location of the next patch of fine turf and the position of the flock at that moment, and even the earliest players preferred holes that required consummate shot making. These shepherds initially gave no thought to competition, but anyone who loves the game enough to play it alone will aspire to glorious accomplishment. Golf is not simply hitting a ball over a particular stretch of grass. Rather, it is a struggle against our own demons and frailties. The tools and the setting become secondary to the task of testing our limitations until they reveal seemingly irrefutable facts, which in turn become goals to overcome through persistence. We press on, raising first our expectations and then our achievements. Like any invention that life requires, golf is, in this regard, spectacular.

So our shepherds determined early on that one big hit plus a lesser one to the hole didn't lead them too far away from the flock to remain in control. This became the staple, what we know today as a par four.

Such holes were *found* for the competitions, but they remained in play only until the following year's event, when new holes were identified. The original shepherds' loops began with a large area of closely cropped grass to serve as the starting point. From there the players would head out toward another fine patch, down an intermediate open area along what they called the "fair way." From the outbound spread of fine turf to the "fair green," where the hole had been cut, they immediately played back to where they'd started. From the bottom of the hole they would steal a pinch of sand on which to stand the ball, in order to hit in the reverse direction. The first rule of the game, produced in 1744 by the Honourable Company of Gentlemen Golfers in Edinburgh: "Ye shall tee thy bal nae more than one cloob length from the hole." That pinch of sand was cheating at first, but eventually it was accepted for such reasons as lessening divots around the hole and maintaining the depth of the hole itself. These two-hole legs of the ancient shepherds' loop were set on differing points of the compass in order to take advantage of as many angles of wind as possible. And, given that play seldom moved more than 200 yards in any direction, the crowd didn't have to travel far to follow the competition. An eight-hole match, short by today's standards, made each contest an easily comprehensible spectacle.

There were holes all around the region that had been developed for the championships: the wonderful links at Leith, Musselburgh and Carnoustie or on the other side of the world at Prestwick or Troon or what is now Turnberry and hundreds of others uncelebrated by famous events. Some holes were actually beginning to formalize, but the championship venue in this formative era had not yet fully evolved. Each year, perhaps to vary conditions that had contributed to a player's previous victory, the matches were played on new "holes"—named after the goal, the man-made excavation that was the ultimate item of interest at the end of each "fair way," cut into each "fair green."

THE COMPETITION for the player of the year had been going on for more than a century in the 1450s, and once that was settled everyday players were keen to take to those new holes, to match their games against the memorable shots of the competitors. They would then forsake the old holes, which had often been obviated by improvements to the ball or clubs or by more powerful players.

This concept created a new livelihood for a cherished few, not as designers but as "finders" of new natural holes. It was a very small group, consisting of older competitors, various technicians (some of whom focused more on appearance than substance) and, from time to time, a charlatan—who was quickly discarded for the big competitions. A few of these faded because their creations were too demanding even for elite players. Finding difficult holes then was as easy as it is today. But a successful few found holes that responded to the challenge—say, by allowing a safe route to a higher score or a risky route to a lower score. Not many finders could locate these on a regular basis without succumbing to the lure of excess difficulty or the frivolity of holes that merely looked the part but were nothing more than grass. Most important, because finding holes implied superior perceptive powers, there was a true mystique about anyone who did so effectively. Only a few could see things that others missed, using greater imagination and finesse. Finding holes was a cranial rather than physical exercise, and the best finders were held in nearly as high esteem as the best players.

The finder would seek out the most acceptable plots of fine turf, especially those with subtle rolls, pits or hollows nearby. From that point, he would look for the wide patches of fescue and then for sheep shelters in the fringes, or hillocks, or stands of marram grass or gorse—anything that would cause a player to think about how that situation should be approached. The finder cut the holes right before the matches, so they would be fresh, and they intentionally grazed the areas to be played and even stomped out small irregularities on the fair greens and swept away the dung. The home hole was actually four fair greens in one, so it had to be large and of fine-quality turf. This would be primary in a finder's process. Depending on the size and nature of the plot, it could have four holes cut into it for each of the approaches.

So the golf course was a floating sequence, manipulated as people saw fit. The players changed. The locations changed. The weather changed, and occasionally the political scene changed. But the *place* did not. The links were such a magnificent matrix of tactical variety that they allowed the shepherd to face an almost infinite number of challenges without ever deserting his flock. The game didn't begin when a shepherd found a hole that pleased him and upon which he honed those skills. No, this happened over an expanse of both space and time, until fascination had become habit and the game had attracted observers. Golf was an indelible portion of society long before a hole or course was ever formalized.

Distant Vision

THE YEAR WAS 1456. A tall young man of eighteen gazed across the expanse of links toward the cold North Sea, less than half a mile away. The sun was at his back, casting a long shadow across the waving tan grasses before him—a foreboding shadow, he thought. A woolen cloak was gathered about him, his usual protection against the winds that constantly blasted this stretch of the coast. His focus was northwest along that coast, of a vision just four miles from where he stood. A dark and unnatural texture covered the land, very different from the rolling pastures at his feet. The scene in the distance appeared to be some great turmoil, with smoke billowing from hundreds of buildings clustered into almost untenable proximity, teeming with people who stepped over running sluices of raw sewage and dodged carts full of various goods. Slovenly hooded figures milled about in all directions, on every manner of mission. Occasionally a figure on horseback or in a carriage moved through the crowds: a noble, official or merchant dressed in bright robes and wearing a hat sporting plumes or fur, denoting privilege. The darkness in the distance was civilization, and above it rose a bright and gleaming edifice that seemed to defy gravity, suggesting that more than human hands had fitted each carved boulder into this colossal mass that floated like a silvery cloud above the dark matrix. The earth where Caeril Patersone stood was pristine, whereas what he saw in the town of St. Andrews was earth layered with a thousand years of filth, sins and blood. But Caeril had come to love that place. It was the home of the championship.

His home, Boarhills, was named after an ancient swine cult, and the prolific wild boar was depicted on the city crest of St. Andrews. The village was but a small curling road laid out by some forgotten Pictish chieftain who here had plotted parcels of land for the dwellings of his subjects. The south end of the street was near the great bend of the Kenly Waters, a stream whose headwaters emerged more than fifteen miles inland, and this was where the settlement had drawn its water for thousands of years. Boarhills nestled cozily about a hundred feet above sea level. On either side were sandy links, lush with fescue and bentgrass and literally covered with sheep.

In centuries past, tradesmen and women purveyed goods and often turned the street entrance to their shelters into a kind of storefront. In 1456, Boarhills was a small but bustling commercial center, dealing in woven goods, raw materials, meat, fish, utensils, footwear and other essential items. Having nearly everyone caught up in trade made the region progressive and financially stable.

Caeril's own contribution was his ancient and indelible lineage of shepherding. But his mind was far from Boarhills and dwelled on his father, who had died in battle exactly a decade before this blustery day, and as his eyes focused on the horizon of the sea he was anguishing over a much more recent event that he feared would change his life no less.

A competition golfer, Caeril had just suffered a loss in the regionals, though not at the hands of a more deft player; at least he didn't think so. No, he had defeated himself. His opponent, John Brighte, was a burly farm boy of twenty-six from Crail, just five miles to the south. He'd been to the championship twice and defeated Caeril several times when the shepherd was younger and less experienced. But on this day, Caeril's conviction had done him in.

The matches followed the eight-hole format, and at the end of regulation they were tied. Caeril's shot with his play-club on the first extra hole flew into tall fescue. In his intensity as he addressed the ball, it rolled back onto the clubface of his mid-iron. His mind exploded in horror: His ball had *moved;* this was a *penalty.* Brighte's ball was on short grass and was not likely to run into trouble. Caeril, staring down, beginning to flush, finally stepped back and then was noticed by the official from the United Golf Honours Society, which accompanied all regional events.

"Aye, Caeril!" he called. "What's the problem, lad? Let's play on."

Caeril just stared at the ground. Then he looked at the official and said softly, "It moved."

"It *moved*?" said the official. "Well, if it moved back to where it was, just play on."

"Nae," said Caeril, "it dinna go back to where it was. It moved."

John walked over and looked at the ball and then at Caeril, with a quizzical expression and a hint of a smile, as if expecting this was some sort of joke.

Now the official was staring down at the ball, though there was no way he could tell if it had moved or not.

"It . . . *moved,*" Caeril said again, even more softly, knowing he must declare an infraction on himself.

"Ah," Brighte said, in a burst of sportsmanship, anxious to get on with it, "just play on, Caeril. We dinna see it."

"I canna," he said. "I saw it move."

John rolled his eyes, and then the official asked Caeril if he wanted to call a penalty on himself, add a stroke and possibly throw away a chance at the championships. "Are ye sure, lad?" he said in a fatherly tone, with Brighte listening.

"Aye," Caeril answered after a long pause, knowing exactly what this amounted to. He was done.

"Patersone plays the odd," said the official, notifying the gallery that something had happened and they were no longer *playing the like,* equal in shots.

Caeril addressed the ball again, this time being very careful, and lofted it onto the corner of the fair green. This raised John Brighte's eyebrows, but he had no trouble getting his ball inside of Caeril's.

Caeril's first roll hit the hole, but with too much speed, and finished several feet beyond. Then John left his on the very edge, literally staring down into the darkness.

"Pick it up, John," said Caeril, his head now spinning with conflicting thoughts.

Brighte looked at the official, who shrugged, but John didn't seem willing to pick up his ball. So Caeril picked up his own ball, which finalized the decision.

John, his ball still lying on the lip of the hole, walked forward to extend his hand in condolence. "I dunna understand what ye just did or why," he said.

"Nor I, John, but I couldna ignore it."

Micael Carrick, Caeril's boyhood companion and clubman (not yet known as a caddie), did understand and was quick to comfort his friend. But others watching the match were not as complimentary, and those who had a groat or two on the outcome scoffed and strode off annoyed, one of them kicking at the sandy soil as he reluctantly handed over his wager.

As Caeril and Micael walked back to the church, the official caught up with them. "I'll be sure the society learns of yer honesty, Caeril," he said. "Too bad all our players aren't as forthright. We'll see to it ye're properly recognized—thanked, ye know?"

Caeril stopped abruptly in his tracks, then slowly looked up with an expression of fierce pain. "Thank me? For what? For not *stealin'*, then, is that it? It's the *rules*. I won't be needin' yer thanks for that." And he strode off in long-legged silence, head down, alone.

Even in his disappointment, Caeril knew he would go to St. Andrews over the next few weeks to watch the matches, where eight players from all over Scotland would play for recognition as the champion. John Brighte would be competing and he himself would not. Still, he found not only the golf but also the events surrounding it irresistible. Great crowds would follow the play, officials parading along with each pairing, and there would be reunions with friends and competitors. He would drink in all the other sights: the cathedral, the bishop's magnificent castle, the churches and universities, the nobility and pilgrims of every station visiting from around Europe. He would undoubtedly agonize that it might have been him in the matches, but he reasoned that somehow it would do him good to see it all happening.

He had been but a small boy of nine on his first visit to the championship, invoking his mother's wrath while his father was in the fields with the flocks. Caeril had spent the full day following the matches, returning home only after dark.

"I was watchin' 'em play, Ma! Ye shoulda seen 'em! Ball flyin' off so far ye canna believe it!"

"To bed! Glory, Caeril, a fright, ye gave me! I'd given ye up for *dead.*"

"Nae, Ma," he had said prophetically, eyes aglow, "I'm *alive*!"

Angus Gille-Copain

THE FIRST FOUR of the seven matches were played on the next-to-last Sunday of February. The two semifinals would be played the following Sunday, the final match a week later, usually before a great crowd. The church not only allowed the competition but promoted it. On Sunday, historically a time of relaxation and attention to the church, meals were often taken there and games were played in the yard throughout the day. It was the church's way of reaching out—or else, as some argued, an attempt to expand its control.

Early on Saturday morning, February 21, 1456, Caeril began his trek to St. Andrews, along the west side of Kittock's Den by the slough that emptied into the sea at an ancient fort Caeril knew nothing about, though his animals frequently grazed around its ruins. The clear morning would be great for the matches, he thought, as he passed the Rock and Spindle, a standing stone placed by his forebears, and then the Kinkell Cave, moving toward the smoke that wafted out over the sea, the prevalent wind direction on kind days.

In half an hour he arrived at the East Sands, a beach near the harbor and below the Mill Port, one of six entrances to the city. He passed under the twenty-foot stone arch, marveling at the immensity of the cathedral as he walked through the grounds. Tomorrow, students and townspeople would be strolling about the cathedral yard and the piers, some playing a stick and ball game of the poor called shintie. By midday there would be but four players remaining. Caeril was already drinking in the festivities.

He went through the Pends, the great covered gate of the south cathedral wall, and found himself at the apex of the three main streets—North, South and, in the center, Merkagait—where the usual Saturday crowd was milling about with oxen and hand carts, pausing at makeshift stands here and there, the street market in full swing. In these three streets, for a price, he could have obtained anything: shoes, a new knife, shears, a robe or tunic, leggings, leather goods, food, both hot and cold, and even quick standing satisfaction in an alleyway with one of the local whores.

On Sunday there would be fewer people on the streets, and they would be trundling toward one of the many churches or the cathedral. Most preferred the smaller churches, like Holy Trinity on South Street, where Caeril would go in the morning before the match. Services at the cathedral were almost overwhelming; for most, Trinity was closer and its size friendlier and more to their taste. But above all, Caeril wanted to hear Bishop James Kennedy, a friend to all and held in a reverence that Kennedy himself steadfastly dismissed. Everyone knew this frail little man with his bald head and great nose, the beloved Old Lord who always dressed in pedestrian garb. Trinity would be packed. People always wanted to hear what this teacher of kings had to say, and on this occasion he would conduct the early, or prime, mass for the competitors, as was the tradition. Afterward, the finalists and their clubmen would march to the golf course, leading a procession of spectators, eliminated players and officials, seemingly the entire tournament.

Caeril, though not particularly devout, briefly stepped in at Trinity for morning prayer, perhaps as much out of guilt as commitment, knowing this would make him more comfortable for the day than if he'd passed by the church without going in. Back out on the street, he saw numerous people moving toward the links.

Caeril enjoyed the Saturday practice, taking in everything and only occasionally wincing at the memory of his self-inflicted elimination. He particularly enjoyed it when an official stepped forward to give a ruling. The players knew the rules, but the officials claimed their presence was required, thus earning these few high-ranking citizens a place in the biggest matches of the year. The players no more needed watching than the Augustinians needed coaching on scripture, but the price they made the officials pay for this entertainment was brutal: the solemn stare of two wary experienced competitors, just waiting for a wrong answer to pounce. In golf, in such ways, the structure of society seemed to wither away.

Caeril studied the traits and strategies of these finalists, imagining himself in their particular situations and marveling at their complex and creative responses to each new problem. Some he knew well, like Brighte, but others he'd never seen before. Every year the competition was becoming more and more intense.

. . .

He spent the night with Micael Carrick at the home of one of Micael's uncles, and in the morning the three of them joined the large crowd outside Trinity and found seats toward the back. The church was nearly full, and Caeril had trouble seeing around a large crop of white hair in front of him as he craned to find the players, who usually sat in the second row on the right, away from the pulpit on the lectern side of the small nave. At this moment his disappointment was acute. He hoped against hope that eliminating himself had not been a fatal mistake, fretting that he might have missed his sole opportunity, that something in the coming year would preclude his chances for 1457. But he was pleased at least to be present, among those who would endure the anguish, including one joyous soul who for twelve months would be known to all as the champion golfer. Caeril had no notion of who aside from Brighte and the official knew of his decision, but in fact nearly everyone did, and no one was surprised to see him at Holy Trinity. The general assumption was that his great moral conviction had been forged in the church, whereas in truth his reverence and conviction were reserved for the game that so permeated his life. His presence in the final eight had been fully anticipated by everyone except himself, so his decision was a topic of much discussion.

As the droning of the liturgy dwindled to the benediction, the players fidgeted. The matches had already been arranged, and in these short days they wanted to make the most of the daylight. On the final amen, they literally bolted out the door, down a small lane, left on Merkagait Street, right on to another path and left again on North Street, which became the lane to the links and the ancient bridge at the Swilken Burn, constructed nearly three hundred years earlier to accommodate commercial traffic between the town and the fishing base on the Eden River estuary beyond the links.

Caeril wanted to run and keep up, but once he cleared the great oaken door of the church someone called his name. "Patersone!"

He didn't recognize the voice and turned reluctantly to see a tall husky man walking toward him, dressed in a short cloak, several layers of muslin shirts, leggings and laced leather shoes. What was most noticeable, however, was the great full head of pure white hair, which had blocked Caeril's view in the church. Though nearing sixty, the man was still healthy, with a friendly round face and a broad smile, and he carried a five-foot staff painted black and white, with a bright red pennant on top. This was Angus Gille-Copain, the legendary finder who set up the shepherds' loops for the championships. Caeril had heard as much about him as he had of any of the players. "Aye, sir," he replied, looking longingly at the quickly disappearing crowd.

"My name is Gille-Copain. I wanted to meet ye to shake yer hand, say hello and talk a spell."

"Aye," Caeril said, extending his hand. "I dinna know 'twas ye in the church. We've never met, though I been watchin' ye since I was a wee lad."

"Ye're *still* a lad, Caeril, but not so wee anymore," he said, smiling.

Caeril smiled back but could not hide his anxiousness.

"Ye'll nae miss a moment of the festivities, Patersone. For sure, they canna begin without me," Gille-Copain said, as he patted him on the shoulder. "Let's walk, then. We can talk on the way. They'll wait."

Caeril was surprised Gille-Copain knew him and was honored that he should seek him out for conversation. Had he known the subject, though, Caeril might have opted not to stop.

"Now, Caeril," Gille-Copain began as they strode along at a good clip, "I'm as confounded as the rest not to see yer name in the lineup for the day. Yet what ye did, callin' that penalty—well, it's unique, eh?"

"I tell ye, sir, disappointed I was—and am yet."

"Well, it is as it should be, but that's only temporary. Ye'll be here in a year, sure, or the next. Ye have what it takes, lad."

Eyeing him, Caeril could tell he was sincere and was comforted that his understanding of the event differed considerably from that of the referee.

"Don't be down, lad. Yer game is fine, and ye'll have yer time. Just keep the edge. Don't stop believin' ye can, Caeril, and stay sharp."

Caeril slowed to look at him.

Gille-Copain met his stare with the most sympathetic expression. "It's sure as mornin'," he continued, "unless ye give up. Dunna do that, lad."

Caeril, taken aback, thanked him, and they resumed their march, making small talk and discussing the matches. Though he would much rather have been playing, Caeril was thrilled to be talking with this icon, having no idea it would lead to a friendship of many years.

Over the next hours he was transfixed by the crowds: their levels of anticipation and their complete awe of the talent before them. He knew the players' traits suggested their personalities; particularly when either struggling or enjoying a success, one's nature is revealed. For Caeril, pining to be in the hunt, the exposure of his psyche was merely a price to be paid. He was ready, and throughout the day Gille-Copain's encouraging words echoed in his mind as he watched the master more closely than ever—holding his staff, pennant flying in the fair way so the players could see the line, leaning it toward the safe side or, on the fair green, resting its base in the hole. But mostly he noticed the ingenious strength of Gille-Copain's mind. The competitors loved and hated him at once, discerning in his creations such imaginativeness that he might have been one of them himself. They sometimes feared the diabolical hazards he found, but they always knew, when the matches were over, that he was nothing if not fair. Only in their own failings did they feel his wrath.

Whatever Gille-Copain's weaknesses had been as a player, he more than made up for them afterward. He was kind and equally encouraging to all—a sort of father figure for the game itself. But what he did best was find golf holes. His knowledge was so real, so introspective, that he could produce brilliant challenges over the links, risks whose rewards included a shorter distance to the hole, a better angle, even a better stance and sometimes all three. He soon became the chosen finder for the championships. He never relied on tricks or deception. His hazards were visible, so players could understand the shot before hitting it; they had only to execute, which is the crux of the game. Gille-Copain brought much to the game but even more to its participants.

Lessons

THE CONVERSATION with Gille-Copain had separated Caeril from Micael, and as it was their practice to follow the matches together, he occasionally looked around for him, anticipating his companionship. Caeril was a superb athlete, trim, quick and rugged, but Micael made him seem like a child.

Micael was a forester, a hunter, having apprenticed with his father and uncles in bringing game to the fleshers, who prepared the take for sale or barter. Only Micael could leave Caeril far behind in a footrace, and he possessed two other traits that were sometimes disconcerting to those who knew him. His family encouraged him from a very young age to make bows, and both boy and bow kept growing more powerful. At his maturity, Micael's longbow was so stiff that no normal man could hope to draw it, and his arrows flew from it with such speed, such flat trajectory, as guaranteed deadly accuracy. No less disconcerting was his incredible stealth. With total control of his body, he could move through any terrain without making a sound, for the hearing of the animals he tracked—deer, wild boar, rabbit—was many times more sensitive than that of man. When Micael wished to remain undetected by men he was literally invisible, and often gave the unsettling impression of having appeared out of thin air—as he did this Sunday afternoon at his friend's side.

Caeril jumped. "Aye, Micael, ye never fail to give me a start. Where did ye get off to?"

"Around," was all he said.

Micael was never one for small talk, though the two of them had spent many hours philosophizing from earliest boyhood, particularly after Caeril's father died at the River Sark. Micael became as a second son to Caeril's mother, both boys comforting her through their mutual grief, an experience that bonded them for life. Micael was Caeril's clubman, but in return Caeril served as Micael's second at his archery meets. In fact, Micael had edged ahead of his friend in that regard, already at nineteen twice the champion of Fife. To their fellows they made an ominous pair, encouraging, coaching and enjoying each other's talents while feasting on everybody else's.

Together they took in the matches, commenting cryptically back and forth, and were excited to see the quarterfinalists finally identified: Nectan MacGregor, John Brighte, Adam Paternis and Baithin Douglas. The celebrants departed with the remaining daylight to play shintie, to talk, to eat and drink in the cathedral close, in keeping with the church's traditional Sunday outline. And once the day had gone dark, a somewhat smaller crowd was drawn away to the less gracious environs of the taverns on Market and North streets.

. . .

WITHIN THE HOUR, a lone man pushed through the loosely hinged door of Tippin's. Eyes turned, man after man, and those who were exchanging greetings parted handshakes and saluting waves as Angus Gille-Copain walked toward the many lamps and candles at the bar. A celebrated figure, Gille-Copain perched on a stout three-legged stool on the elbow of the bar and the establishment owner, Eldon Tippin, quickly placed what he knew to be his favorite libation before him: half a pewter cup of single-malt whisky. This was all Gille-Copain would drink for the next two hours, while holding the crowd spellbound. Golf matches had been played for almost a century now, and Gille-Copain had seen nearly half of them.

The rafters of the low ceiling were logs stripped of their bark, and numerous oil lamps cast a golden hue throughout the small room. The bar itself was a highly polished slab of oak, nearly a yard wide and some fifteen feet long, with a slight curve. Tippin valued width above straightness but had rounded and smoothed the edges to spare his patrons the splinters. Tonight the house was full, some standing at the bar, others sitting at small tables on shorter stools or the odd chair. The room was aglow with a dim, golden light.

After some idle conversation about the day's matches, one of the eight finalists, Samsone MacLeod, from distant Applecross Forest in the West Highlands, asked a favor of Gille-Copain concerning beginnings of the game.

"Would ye tell it again? There's many a new ear to hear, and the old ones would welcome it too."

Silent anticipation filled the room. Frowning slightly, Angus reminded everyone the story was only that, just a story. Then, raising his eyebrows and looking down, he said, "Or is it?"

At once all attention was fixed on him.

"It's of a place we all know well, in the links, maybe these right here at St. Andrews, but ye know, it's hardly likely some lad just up and invented golf. It's a game so simple and natural that it gradually came about on its own time. Maybe it was a shepherd like Samsone or young Patersone here"—motioning to a suddenly beaming Caeril—"tendin' his sheep when he chanced on a round pebble. And havin' his crook in his hand, he *struck it awa*!" Gille-Copain made a short fierce swing from his stool. "For it is inevitable that a man or lad with a *stick* in his hand should aim a blow at any loose object lyin' in his path, as natural that he should *breathe*."

There were chuckles around the room.

"On pastures green this led to naught. But in the links-lands, once upon a time, probably that shepherd rolled one of those stones into rabbit scrape. 'Marry,' he quoth, 'I couldna do that if I tried.' It was a thought so instinctive to his ambition that nerved him to the attempt in the first place. But nae man nor lad will long persevere alone in any arduous task, so our shepherd hailed another, who was hard by, to witness this endeavor, who said, 'Forsooth! 'Tis easy!' And tryin' "—a moment's hesitation—"he failed!"

The room burst into laughter, and Angus bowed his head slightly.

"More!" called several listeners. "More!"

"Failed?" Angus asked, looking around at each face. He was smiling, eyes gleaming, face brightly alive. "We play *not* to fail, lads. But hittin' the stone *in* the hole from a distance calls out for divine help, true?"

There was a collective mumble of agreement.

"Do we play lookin' for that master stroke? Aye, of course we do, but with the mere size of the ball and the hole, and the wind and the slope and the sun in our eyes, the noises we hear or the rain or the cold, our opponent or partner, even a little nick on our finger, we play just to get it *close.* But once in a great while the unseen spirit that wills a lightnin' bolt just to balance the cosmos will send one *into* the hole. We're the lucky benefactors, lads. In it goes, we cheer, and on we play."

The room was completely silent.

"It's just a game," he said, "but somehow, lads, it's worked its gleamin' magic into our very souls." He took a *scalch* from his mug, a wee nip, and sat for a long moment with his head bowed, looking at the earthen floor covered with dried grass. The others remained as silent as parishioners before the prayer. Angus's head slowly began to rise until, his eyes firmly closed, he seemed to be looking through the rounded rafters at some vision in another medium altogether. Then, almost in a whisper, the elders straining to hear, he continued.

" 'Twas eons before the Romans, yet they, our very fathers, were here." He opened his eyes and looked at them, their gazes in turn fixed on him. "When ye walk the links, the sand and dust ye kick about yer feet are from ancient times. *They* are there, yer father's father's father's father, and on and on, and when *their* dust was flesh on these same lands they roamed with their woolly charges, and their tedium was thick, those with any mind at all. It was a struggle just to make the day move on. The boredom dulled their very wits.

"One fine day, a round black jetstone rolled off a shepherd's fingers onto a gentle slope. Down it went, smooth, across the fresh-grazed fescue. It turned this way and that"—he motioned with his hand—"and then caught the glint of a bright mind as it came to a stop at the bottom. It was on *that* day, lads, hundreds of years even before Jesus came to Bethlehem, that the shepherd set the roll loose for the first time. And God knew at that *exact* moment that He would send an angel to watch over our fathers. He knew we were strugglin', aye, nearly *blind* from boredom with the sheep. And so did the angel know we needed food for our weary minds; somethin' to occupy us whilst stayin' close by creatures that was ours *and* his.

"And that young lad, he said aloud, with the stone lyin' now at the bottom of the slope, 'What was that? Only a stone, it is, but why can't I walk away? I'll do it again.' And so he took his crook and nudged it a bit, then struck it harder, and before long he knew he would move it *only* with that crook. He turned it end for end, to strike with the top of the staff, where he could put the flat side to the stone and launch it on the line he intended.

"That angel the good Lord gave us, he was there in the links with that shepherd, hearin' every bleat but doin' his job of freein' that lad's mind by the magic of the roll. It wasn't much, was it? But look what it has *become.* Before long, just to make it better, the angel whispered in that shepherd's ear, 'Make it harder,' just as *we* do. 'Make it test me and I'll do it! Take me away!'

"The shepherd sees a route that passes hard by a sandy path. It must nearly kiss that path or it'll not have enough borrow to reach that small spot in the turf where he's pulled out some baby gorse. The staff comes back with both hands and strikes it firm along the line to the edge of the path—seven, maybe eight steps away—but just before it drops into that sand it borrows on the slope and curves away. The lad sees every turn, every little change magic to him as it rolls past that trouble into new land, toward his spot but still well left. It's beyond his control, but why is he still connected? And ye know the answer, lads. That line was *his* line and that stone is *him,* rollin' along over that tight silver turf."

Angus stood and motioned with his hands. "Now the stone's goin' from his left to his right, and our lad starts movin' to his left. Why? I do it too! We *all* do. His staff's in his hand, the crook pointed up as he sees it goin' for the mark, body tense, curlin' lips, teeth showin', jaw clenched tight, eyes a-squintin' as the stone rolls slower and slower but holds the line. Then, with one bitter last turn, it comes to rest—well, lads, don't you know—right *on* that spot!" His arms shot into the air and his head flew back as he let loose a startling shriek.

Everyone in the room jumped.

Angus slowly lowered his arms and looked from man to man, beads of perspiration now glistening on his temple. "And he's *hooked,* lads. That first lad, aye, he was taken in by the roll. He was the first—well, he was the first of *us*! And he will continue on to do it time and again, hours on end, makin' a game of it, lookin' always for that nice round stone.

"The roll became fixed in his life, by his almost mad desire to see it again. Then it passed from father to son, unendin' generations mindin' the sheep, from father to all the sons of Abraham, sharin' like brothers that common ground, century after century, that garden of wilderness we know as the links, caught up in the mystery of rollin' and then flyin' stones into those glorious slopes and that hard-leanin' wind—a fire they'd never see put out. And so the game was begun."

The silence in the tavern was complete until a man rose from his stool to address the assembly, appearing peculiarly out of place. Well dressed and strikingly handsome, Colaim Cummings was a lawyer with the Justiciary, the high court in Perth. Yet he was one of them still. He'd been eliminated earlier in the day, but in fact Colaim was the only man to win all the major events in a single year, and in the past fourteen he'd taken the championship three times. He had told his fellow competitors on many occasions that he preferred their company to that of his more privileged colleagues, which Colaim's wife knew to be all too true. And now, in barristerial form, he commanded the floor with Angus Gille-Copain as his star witness, seated again at the corner of the bar.

"My learned colleague," he told him, "it appears the jury has the need for yet more facts from your vast and eloquent musings on our game. Might you relate more, which might prepare us for the festivities forthcoming and for our dreams these nights while Nectan, Adam, Baithin and John suffer fitful sleep—a discomfort we all here would barter for a place in the proceedings come Sunday's dawn?"

And with that Samsone MacLeod, the common shepherd, spoke again, now in a mockingly quizzical tone. "What'd he say, then?"

To a man they all roared with laughter, which graduated into applause, with Samsone bowing theatrically toward Colaim.

"I believe," Colaim said to Angus, after returning the bow, "that my esteemed compatriot joins me in bidding you to continue." Grinning, Samsone shook his hand, and Colaim gave him an affectionate one-armed hug and added, with a sweeping wave of his other arm, "But only after our host has served another round, and it will be on *my* tab."

Enthusiastic applause followed, and after every mug had been refilled, they sought their places and settled in.

Angus's voice rose in the silence. He told them of Pytheas, a Greek adventurer from Marsalla who came ashore near Fife Ness "more than a thousand years ago," from out of a haar, the dense, cold and windless mist particular to this part of the world, needing to replenish supplies on his ship. The frightened tribesmen thought he was Llyr, the old pagan god of the sea. Angus painted a picture of a tall, hoary and powerful man who presented them with gifts. The tribesmen joined in the hunting and gathering and watched in wonder as Pytheas, at highest noon, used a knotted length of string and the shadow of his staff to determine what he called latitude of this place.

In the sand on the edge of the sea, there was, Angus explained, a great gap between those who knew the earth was round and where they were on it, and others who knew only to keep their boats within sight of land or be lost forever. Pytheas, one of the former, even kept a record—*On the Ocean,* it was called—that Greek and Roman historians quoted from regularly in their works, but, alas, the book perished in the great fire in ancient Alexandria.

The group stirred. To them, the notion of a round earth was monumental. They had all considered what they were seeing as they looked out from the shore and fished in the sea, and some had heard the earth described as a globe. Still, it would be another thirty-six years before Christopher Columbus garnered the money and courage to seek the western route to India for Queen Isabella of Spain.

Angus told them that Pytheas's crew brought ashore a collection of flat-ended sticks and wooden balls, which they batted about on the beach, three against three, trying to hit the ball over a line at either end of a quickly defined pitch. These tribesmen were being introduced to a civilization far in advance of their own, and in exchange for the locals' goodwill and assistance, Pytheas left behind a few trinkets, amber from Jutland and tin from Cornwall, along with two of the sticks and two of the balls.

"Could it have been? Sticks and balls, eh?" Angus took another sip from his mug, slapped his thighs and said, "Lads, I'll have a pee," and stepped outside.

. . . .

Barely an hour had passed since Angus's arrival at Tippin's, and in his absence conversation revived. A young man named William, still aglow from hearing about "the roll," had a question fixed in his mind about the spot on the ground. Even before Angus closed the door and came back inside, he asked, " 'Tis a poor question, but how came we to the hole? In those days was it nae a mere scrape?"

Gille-Copain, once situated, looked at the young lad and drew a deep breath. "Nae, William, 'twas *not* a scrape. It's been some time since anyone asked about the hole. It dunna cross many minds, but it's a story that matters to our kind. It was just after we chased the Romans off Hadrian's Wall, and even so we dinna like each other much back then, so there was many tiffs round the land. But the shepherds stayed mostly in the links and fields, tendin' and rollin'. But ye know, lads, the best thing the Romans left us was a ball, that leather pouch now stuffed with feathers but early on just with Roman hair. They called it the *paganica.* Heavy it was, but it rolled straight, and by that time, after St. Ninian and before St. Columba, some was rollin' balls carved of pine and yew that took considerable time to make. Dinna want to lose *them,* eh?"

Angus pointed out how the first boy cuffed his nice round stone into the rabbit scrape and went to retrieve it, only to discover it was too much work, once it was into the maze of the scrape, to dig it out. After that, when he had a nice round stone, he tried *not* to hit it into a scrape and played *away* from the hole. He then explained that for many years the competitions were won by those who could play closest to an object without hitting it. This became a constant source of disagreement and soon threatened the game.

"But there's somethin' about the hole. The *hole,*" he mused. "What is it?"

They looked at one another, wondering. They had never thought much about the hole.

"Lads." He caught their eyes, one by one. "Clubs are important to ye, and the ball, that goes without sayin'. But without the hole, my friends, there *is* nae game. The hole could be the most important of all. *Finality* is what it gives us. As long as the ball stayed above the ground the result was arguable. But when it fell out of sight, the task was *complete* with nae dispute. Reckonin' which player was closest caused 'em to fight, puttin' a bad spin on our game. So just countin' the strokes till ye was out of sight, that's better—in the bottom of a hole that dinna *eat* the ball. Still, it goes a lot deeper than we know, at least for me, and I'll tell ye why. It's that man needs an end to things."

His manner seemed a bit more serious now, more like a professor or a preacher. "Ye notice that when someone dies, we put 'em in a hole. It's not the hole that makes it final, though, lads. It's putting 'em *in* the hole, seeing 'em disappear. Knowin' when the sand pours over the box and the stone goes up at the head that the body's gone—just a memory. The women cry, us menfolk too sometimes, but it's over. We *need* that. We need to see and know that it's over."

He paused. "I'll say no more on dyin.' But the ball findin' the hole, that's final too. The first in either wins or ties, but the man playin' the odd can't catch up when the other ball falls. No arguin', is there? This game's for gentlemen. We dunna fight. Dunna argue. In the golf as in life, the hole means it's *over.* Cry we might, but that's the end of it. We just make our way to the hole. . . ." He studied the far corners of the tavern, his face somber. "Nae, nae more, lads."

But after another slow sip from his pewter mug, the twinkle returned to his face and his audience seemed relieved. He turned to young William and told him of another young lad, Thomas Dunbar of Berwick. Thomas had tired of the bickering over who was the closest.

"Young Thomas," Angus said, "he'd bring stones from the burn to pitch at the scrapes. Ye understand, he *liked* to see the stone disappear down into the darkness of the hole. And after a time it struck him. *'That's it!'* he said. He set about findin' a fine patch of turf that was just grazed, and there he knelt with his knife to *cut* a hole in that spot!"

Angus shrugged. "It wasna so easy as that, though. At first he made it a wee bit wider than his stone. But when he set to cleanin' it out, he couldna get at it, diggin' with just two fingers. The frustration and his curiosity made him dig it wide enough to put his whole hand in, to scoop out the sand till it was about the same size of a scrape. Down he went, up to his wrist. Then he leaned back and picked up the round stone lyin' by his ankle and with his hand rolled it the short distance over the grass—toward his new idea." He shook his head and smiled. "Lads, when that stone crossed the lip and dropped in with that sound we all know and love, young Tom let loose of a sigh. 'Ahh,' he said, 'that felt good.' So it was Tommy Dunbar who saw the answer: the hole. And here we are, tryin' forever to land ourselves in it."

Angus Gille-Copain then eyed each and every man in Tippin's for several long moments, letting them know that something important was coming. "Sometimes the world changes with the simplest of thoughts. The mind's gyrations are bigger and more powerful than the most eloquent words. The new idea need not be said, only *felt*. Answers explode in the mind in just a blink, and the world might jump forward to a whole new time. Hear me on this, lads. Few things on this earth is more satisfyin' than the birth of an idea that brings a problem to bear. Soon, around Dunbar, every shepherd was rollin' into a hole and they were matchin', they was, man on man. If ye was down in four and the other more, they started sayin' ye'd *won the hole.* Won the *hole,* and it stuck.

"But most of all, there was no more fightin', even when the ball caught the lip, for it was *out;* when it fell after a bit on the lip, it was *in.* When it was struck, it was either in or out. Who *won* was in the strokes. And who was first in the hole was *first up the slope* to roll again. *Ye're up,* the other would say, as we still say today. And if ye're up, ye play first on the next hole. Well, word traveled fast around the links and, before they knew, it went all the way to the Highlands. Shepherds was rollin' to a hole about the size of their hand, and they was countin' *strokes* to the bottom of the hole."

Angus Gille-Copain was again staring at the floor. Somehow, something about this troubled him. "Aye, lads, the hole is a dark subject, but it saved our game, it did."

Flyers

THE TAVERN was abuzz with many conversations; then the question of finding holes was put to Gille-Copain. He was quick to say it was very simple, just a matter of locating hazards and smooth turf where the hole could be placed so that players could then take their chances. Though he delivered this message with a big smile, he was daring them to try it, since knowing the fact was one thing while actually *finding* the holes quite another.

"Aye, it's as easy as sculptin' a statue of the king. Take a very large stone and then chip away whatever dunna look like James!"

Colaim Cummings roared along with some, while others just stared dumbly through the haze until more gifted friends explained.

Angus Gille-Copain was indeed an artisan in his daily life, often called upon by barons and officials to provide any manner of painting, sculpture or, as had become his passion in later years, furniture. His pieces, particularly the small tables, were much sought after, all fashioned with unique joinery and exceptional proportion. In his small shop in the fishing village of Anstruther, on the north coast of the Firth of Forth, he employed two guildsmen, one of them his son, and two apprentices, one of them his grandson. He was a master carver and craft was his vocation, but the golf matches were his life.

Meanwhile, Caeril and William and several others were surveying the great slab of oak into which faces had been carved, their subjects slightly caricatured but easily identifiable. There, for posterity, laughing back at all who could see, were Colaim Cummings, Nectan MacGregor, Adam Paternis, Mal-Giric Alexander, Baithin Douglas and others from long ago. There were no names, only the triumphant smiles of men who'd won the championship for going on forty years. Everyone knew how they happened to be there.

Tippin's tavern had long been Gille-Copain's last stop after the championship before he headed south to Anstruther, and—in what was by now a ritual—when Tippin himself placed food and a pewter of malt on the bar before him, he also brought a candle and a straight stick of ash. After dinner, Angus would burn the top of the ash and begin evoking an image of the day's victor right on the surface of the bar as he ate, sometimes referring to dogged-edged pieces of parchment on which he'd made small sketches. Repeat winners needed only a new date carved below their faces. The burnt ash would move with the purpose and efficient simplicity of an expert, and there, often in just a few minutes, a new champion would be awaiting immortality. Angus would then pay the barman, shake his hand, bid him good night and pat Rufus Burns, once his apprentice, on the shoulder. Rufus would sit down immediately on Angus's stool, unroll a leather strip full of neatly pocketed razor-sharp carving tools and begin to turn the charcoal sketch into a relief, as he and Angus had done with the other faces—as well as nearly every religious artifact and architectural accent for the Augustinians in the cathedral. Within an hour, the new carving was being doused with oil and vigorously rubbed to create the same patina as on the others, save a little lighter. It was a thing of beauty, but just as striking was the fact that this giant curving slab of oak still had room for at least another fifty winners. Many who came to the tavern were comforted to know there was plenty of space left.

Then John Brighte moved to the corner of the bar and, in a brief lull, spoke with the halting inelegance of his farming trade. His was a question that would surprise no one in the room. John was unchallenged as the longest hitter of the day, though his colossal length was, if anything, less impressive than the elegant short game he used to back it up.

"Ye've told us of the roll and the hole," he said, "but how did we get off the ground? What happened to put the ball in the air?"

"Aye, Johnny," Angus responded with a grin, "but why should *ye* be askin' such a question?"

This brought laughter and much ribbing, and Brighte looked offended until he registered that everyone was merely acknowledging his prodigious length. He then smiled and feigned a backhand slap at his barmate, who pulled back, laughing.

"Well," John Brighte said, "I was just wonderin', ye know. Is there a story, then?"

"It's a good question, John, no doubt, and it happened back when our forebears, yers and Nectan's—the Angles with yer own yellow hair and blue eyes—decided to go on a rampage. They had two kings, Oswiu first and then Ecgfrith, after Oswiu died. Ecgfrith was the one we Picts hated most. He took Dysart and Kirkcaldy, where the Picts made iron. They had all that coal too." He gestured at the overflowing coal box by the hearth. "So the Angles had Galloway and Dumfries, near all of the south, maybe eight hundred years ago."

By the fifteenth century, most everyone in the room had been exposed to books and reading, though many nobles, for numerous devious reasons, were not keen on educating commoners. But this story was national legend, told generally by fathers and mothers to their young.

"Ecgfrith was wicked," he continued. "He set upon the Picts like they was animals but made 'em keep on with the smelting. Twelve or thirteen years later, the Picts banded secretly together and swore to throw off the yoke of slavery, so they made themselves some swords and spears and faced Ecgfrith at a place called the Plain of Manaw. It was a terrible mistake, lads. Our band was cut up bad, and news traveled north that Ecgfrith was not yet done—that he was marching north, sensing that all the Lowlands could be his. But Ecgfrith woulda been better off stayin' put. He dinna know what was happenin' just outside Montrose. And if he had, he nae woulda marched—nae, never."

This vivid introduction had tweaked everyone's interest, and most suspected Angus would spin a version they never before had heard.

"There was a band of lads near Montrose, young men, actually, though most not yet twenty. They had but one trait in common, that of size. Now, lads, they were nae big like Johnny there," he said, pointing at the burly Brighte. "They was big like ye see just once in a great while, makin' our John look a ragamuffin."

He went on to explain that those who weren't tall were burly, but that most were both tall *and* burly, with bare arms and necks like stumps that went from just below their ears right to their lumpy shoulders. They had powerful legs, with bulging calves, raw hands, wild beards, and such hair that only headbands could hold it back. Scariest of all, their faces were scarred, often disfigured, from the rough life. They were brutes. At first there were just a few, a rough lot, working the lord's fields, quibbling over the smallest things. But they were good proud workers, each bearing the load of two or three men. Out of pent-up energy and frustration, they regularly held contests to see who could lift the most, or push the most or pitch the farthest. Before long, other big boys showed up, having heard of the group by word of mouth.

They came from all around, some all the way from Samsone's country, in the Highlands, a particularly fierce breed. They were formidable. Many had or used horses too, all shires, as big, heavy and strong as the men themselves.

What brought them together now was that to a man they were dissidents, deeply upset that their own families lacked the will or spirit to take on Ecgfrith. This sat so poorly with them they wanted nothing to do with everyday folk. When not working the fields, they were a roaming, dusty cloud of ill-tempered bullies, barely within the constraints of the law. They thought themselves rebels, whereas the locals considered them hooligans and gave them a wide berth. It was practically a throwback to the times of ancient tribes.

But like all boys, they had one incurable eternal weakness: girls. Still, they appeared so mean that parents sheltered their daughters and kept them well clear. The boys didn't go to church either, but on Sundays they would peer through the marram grass as the girls went rolling in the links with their families.

"Ah, maybe it was the times, or just lads bein' lads, but they was wantin' the lassies so much they was beginnin' to twitch."

There were snickers in the crowd.

Angus said, in a soft lilt, "The lads, they liked rollin' too, but they come to see it as just a little game their parents played on Sundays, and they couldna join in. To their thinkin', their fathers was spineless for not kickin' Ecgfrith out of their land. But, as much as they couldna abide Ecgfrith, they dinna want to be Picts either. Given that, not only was they big, they was barkin' mad, hardly a good combination.

"They made up their own games in the links, wrestlin' or just fightin' in intense displays of strength, always lustin' after the lassies. Still, they knew that just takin' 'em would bring the lord's knights down on them, and though they liked the idea of that fight, it would likely be the end of them.

"Then one day it happened. One of them was lyin' on the back crest of a dune, spyin' through the fescue on a beautiful creature who was rollin' with some friends. He evidently reached his limit and lost control, slidin' down the dune in a fit of rage and prepared to attack the first human or animal he encountered. But all he could find was his rollin' club. His face drawn up like a clenched fist, he thought instantly of rendering it asunder, but instead, and for no reason whatsoever, he threw down a feathery ball and smashed it as hard as he could. It took off like a comet. Other lads saw it go and, sufferin' the same illness, struck away as well. In just moments, balls was flyin' everywhere. As soon as they found them, they hit again and yet again. Balls filled the sky, some explodin' in great clouds of feathers. A few shafts splintered, but in their frustration the lads kept on, launchin' both shots and themselves into somethin' new.

"And, lads, ye'll like this part." Angus paused for effect. "Every lass on the far side of the dune saw the balls flyin' and, before long, was standin' up top watchin' in wonder. But—every bit as strange—that's the first time the lassies had seen the lads up close, and they liked what they saw! Sure, it looked a ramblin' mass of tattered rags with great muscles and wild hair, but those flyin' balls was a kind of statement," Angus explained. "*We're different!* they was sayin', each time a ball soared off. But ye know, lads, it mighta been what pleased the lassies most was the frustration, not the strength.

"Think about it. In just a moment, the lads changed from riffraff to manly, and by the end of the day they would have a name, too: the Flyers. What they dinna know, lads, was that within a cycle of the moon they'd become the *immortal* Flyers.

"They strengthened their clubs and, most of all, worked on the ball, makin' it out of tougher hide and more firmly stuffed, with tighter, stronger stitchin'. Their leader was the one who could hit it farthest, and as it happens he was also the meanest, and this bolstered their already storied image. But no matter what the lasses thought, their families would allow them no contact with this group.

"Even if the lads knew the lassies might be willin', they couldna get past the parents. The lads was twitchin' bad," Angus said, "about to explode."

The listeners loved this last bit and wondered where all of this might be going. They didn't have to wait long to find out.

" 'Twas a Friday mornin'," Angus told them, "actually the

nineteenth day of May in 685, as the books record. The unruly Flyers began their march into legend, and our game was the beneficiary."

THE BOYS had been celebrating all night. Their excuse was the old pagan feast of Bel, the god of the underworld and their hero. Now the sun was telling them it was time to head to the fields, and they were dreading the long day ahead. But as they walked along the path to Brechin from the links, a rider appeared, coming at full tilt. True to form, they did not clear the path but held their ground. If the rider wanted to pass, it would be on the Flyers' unflinching terms. But he pulled up just short of them, his face white with terror.

"Ecgfrith! Ecgfrith marched into Forfar!" he shouted. "We need men!"

"Ecgfrith!" the boys muttered, looking at one another as bitter anger erupted in their souls. *"The bastard!"*

The time was right. The very thing they hated most, the root cause of their suffering, was presenting itself, and in this state of mind they were focused on exacting their pound of flesh or, as Scots do, perishing in the effort. At that moment, the Flyers may have been the most powerful force on the face of the earth, man for man. They had neither training nor strategy. All they had and all they would need was hatred, frustration, youth and size. Suddenly transformed into thirty-three fearsome warriors, they were all on horseback within the hour, whether their own animal or one "borrowed," and bolting to the west over fields they knew so well toward Forfar.

Traversing the land, they were unaware there was some fight left in the Picts after all. At that moment, their own King Bridei Mac Bile was in fact gathering an army nearby in the foothills of the Cairngorm mountains. But as far as the Flyers were concerned, in their rage and youthful delusion they were off to stop Ecgfrith by themselves, and within three hours, they reached a meadow north of Forfar.

Ecgfrith had spent the previous night sacking the town, raping, murdering and pillaging. Once the sun was well up, he set out to the north, continuing his drive, and when they stopped just over a hill, ready to make camp, Ecgfrith himself saw the band of mounted men in resplendent brown standing at the far end of the meadow, half a league away.

He turned in his saddle to ask his general, "What's *that?*"

"Dunno," he answered. "Looks like they're carrying sticks!"

"Kill them," Ecgfrith said calmly.

"Aye," said the general, motioning a band of men in that direction.

A company of sixty took off, bent on massacring this ragtag gathering of what appeared to be crofters armed only with clubs. They charged across the meadow, their general in the lead.

But the Flyers stood on their horses like statues, moving not an inch, until, when the Northumbrians came into range, they repositioned and exposed one man with a powerful bow, a joiner who also made their clubs. His bow was as taut as a drawbridge chain, so they say, and the general didn't see him until it was too late; something had penetrated his body and he was falling from his horse. His soldiers were stunned to see him sprawled in the tall fescue, gasping his last before a group of peasants.

Then, to their paralyzing horror, they saw that these were not just men on horses but *huge* men riding *huge* horses, bellowing like animals and now bearing down on them at top speed.

Leaderless, the Northumbrians panicked. Ecgfrith watched in disgust as his soldiers scattered, falling one by one like boys sent to do a man's bidding. Blows from clubs or from mighty muscled arms, delivered from gigantic animals, were cutting down his troops as easily as scythes in a field of hay. Some of the Flyers discarded their clubs for their victims' weapons, chasing down fleeing Northumbrians who, moments later, were lifeless in the grass. Ecgfrith saw one Flyer on foot knock a horse off balance and snuff its rider by breaking him over his knee like a stick. They were possessed; Ecgfrith simply could not believe what he was seeing. When a handful of his men came running back, he dispatched one of them himself with a swipe of his great battle sword, screaming "Coward!" as the headless corpse collapsed at his horse's hooves.

THERE WAS NOT a sound in the room.

"This, lads, was the beginnin' of one of the monumental battles in our history. It would change our very lives, though it was long, long ago."

When that man's head hit the ground, an enraged Ecgfrith bolted forward with his entire army. The Flyers, seeing their charge, knew it was time to move and dashed west, toward the mountains, in a stroke of luck. They didn't know they were leading Ecgfrith directly to King Bridei's horde, which was preparing for attack from over the crest of a hill named Dunnichen.

With a good lead, the Flyers had no trouble; the Northumbrians were already worn out from their march and the previous night's raid and would be even more vulnerable once the boys reached the trees at the end of the field. Off they went across that large meadow, Ecgfrith himself leading the pursuit, but in the heavy foliage of the tree line, the Flyers seemed to melt away, much as their forefathers had done when facing Roman Emperor Septimius Severus about 475 years earlier.

The crowd in the bar was coming to realize that Angus Gille-Copain was a remarkable historian.

"Ecgfrith," Angus continued, "smellin' trouble, halted his troops well short of the trees. And there his army stood, waitin' on Ecgfrith to give the next orders."

In the silent room, Angus's voice commanded everyone's rapt attention as he explained that the Northumbrians, alone in the meadow, were thoroughly spooked. Then through the silence came eerie howls of the Flyers as from a wolfpack, the sound seeming to surround them. In that age, the call of the wolf signified evil and dark magic, and it cast a pall over Ecgfrith's warriors. Actually, the Flyers were just trying to buy some time, but to the surprise of both sides the howl suddenly grew and grew, building into a mighty roar as a literal landslide of Bridei's crisp brigades rushed down the hill into the right flank of the exhausted Northumbrians and smote them absolutely, in a merciless bloodletting. It was over in just an hour. The hated Ecgfrith was left lying lifeless, his blood mingling with that of his troops in a grotesque red stream through the Pictish grass.

"The books tell us 'twas three in the afternoon." Angus then cleared his throat and took a *scalch*. "It was the battle of Dunnichen, lads, a slaughter maybe equal to Robert the Bruce's whippin' of Edward Longshanks at Bannockburn. Sure, we won our independence in that one, but had the Flyers nae been mad and had Bridei nae been ready, mind you, the Bruce wouldna had his chance later on and Scotland never born at all."

And indeed the Flyers were famous, revered throughout the realm, living out their days, playing their flying game in the links. This in time came to be all the rage and they were its masters. These outcasts had brought all of Pictland together, and now their version of golf was the kingdom's treasure. No part of society tried any longer to shun them. And the boys—well, they too were finally all right. The girls they so desired urged the boys to join their flying with the rolling, a natural combination that brought forth on the fine grasses of the mighty links a new, more complex and exciting exercise: bashing the ball as far as the eye could see a time or two, then rolling it into a hole. They gave it a name, too, which persisted still in 1457 and beyond: the Long Game.

"So, Johnny, lad, ye may look like an Angle, but more than any of us ye are a Flyer. That's how our game got into the air. It was pride and ferocious spirit, not to mention a little of the other, eh, lads?" John's face erupted in crimson and those around him patted him on the shoulder. "The game, they put it into the air, then across the grass and into the hole. It's *our* game, then. Been playin' it ever since."

Several men noticed that John Brighte, through this entire tale, had not taken even a sip.

"It's late, lads," Angus advised. "Prime mass next Sunday; we dare not miss it. Kennedy will want to see us there, and we must stay on the good side of our host. Just a week now, and we'll know who it is this year. We'll have fun watchin'." After a slight pause, and with a note of longing in his voice, he added, "But we'd all rather be playin', would we not?"

The players grinned broadly.

"Off with ye now, to sleep."

Players

John Brighte went on to defeat Baithin Douglas in the semifinals, while Nectan MacGregor beat Adam Paternis. In the final match, John outdrove the defending champion, but Nectan's scorching approaches countered his play-club length. On the first extra hole, Brighte made a putt from well outside of MacGregor, who in turn made his for the half. The reverse occurred on the second. Phenomenal matching threes further excited the crowd on the third, only to be followed by embarrassing fives on the fourth, though both players made spectacular recoveries from sand and deep rough. Finally, on the fifth extra hole, the challenger prevailed by holing a deft chip. It was a tremendous match, leaving competitors and spectators alike limp from the intensity.

A year later they were still reliving this great battle. Though journalism was not yet a part of society, every championship produced great matches witnessed by many and retold by the likes of Angus Gille-Copain, and over time these grew into feats of immortal proportions, unencumbered by the finality of the printed word. But now, in February of 1457, the field had once again been reduced to eight players, some of them legendary personalities nearly on a par with barons and bishops with the golf crowd.

Thousands played at golf, but few had the uncanny ability to execute at near-perfect levels for extended periods. The game was measured at bogey and higher, so those capable of moving the ball around in sub-bogey figures or better caught the fascination of the public, much like tumblers or jugglers. Without doubt, this contributed greatly to the game's popularity. Blasting the ball into the heavens with incredible accuracy and consistency, and performing with a magical touch around the fair greens, the men were at least one stroke better than the average player on *every* hole, and they formed a very small group that was revered by those who could only dream. While playing the game was what the gentry liked best, and they enjoyed it as often and for as long as possible, it was the feats of the championship players that set the bar and demonstrated that improvement—if not perfection—was possible.

Meanwhile, a culture evolved around the club itself. What was the best wood for the shaft and the head? What was the preferred loft or material for the grip? And discussion about the ball was never-ending. The ball was variously deemed too fragile, too light, too heavy—when the clubhead shattered—not round enough, or out of balance. Such deliberations were the quest for perfection, if not in playing, which was an impossible goal, then at least in the equipment.

Fierce as they may have been at war, as a race the Scots were generally steadfast, quiet, reserved and conservative. Their natural style was to stifle most outward expression; even when reveling in utmost joy they allowed themselves but a fleeting flash, a grin, a small sound or gesture, and only with appropriate restraint. To be Scottish was not to be solemn, merely silent. When they succeeded, they exploded inside, and when they failed, they quietly destructed, though to the casual observer they would seem to be just enjoying the walk. And they felt, when watching the competitions, a massive subliminal association with the players, each group having an uncanny understanding of the other through shared interests.

Each competitor appealed to varying segments of the public, and many had regular followers. The galleries were usually thick with friends and relatives, but once in a great while there arrived a new player whose persona attracted large numbers of followers, a player whose image and traits spanned the differences of class, locale and even clan, his emotions uncharacteristically obvious, his intentions honest, his competitiveness intense and his honor impeccable. It is interesting that such personalities were excused from typical Scottish conservatism, as though their reactions were an expression for all the land, allowing their galleries vicarious collaboration in their successes and immense empathy in their failures, all of them succumbing totally, in good times or bad, to that player's glowing charisma.

And so a sideline within competition golf was the assessment of the various competitors' characters. Some players invited saintly comparisons, some exacted motherly sentiments from older women, some appealed strictly to the male constitution and some—well, some could quicken a woman's senses. The Scots uncovered the true nature of each man, his individual traits floating to the surface as clear to them as to his own mother. No player could fabricate himself. They were what they were, and in the heat of battle their reality was laid bare.

But they had one spectacular similarity: an uncanny ability to move the ball great distances and quickly into the hole. For the competitors, their goal was to reach the fair green in two blows where they could finish with two strokes over the fine carpet into the hole. That happened reasonably often, but by and large the standard score was five, and they expected to come up short somewhere along the route. The deterrent was almost always a difficult or impossible lie, a common occurrence in the rough terrain of the links, but no one complained about a bad lie. It was, as it has been said, the rub of the green. When the chips were down in the finals, however, the number of strokes taken by the best players tended to be astonishingly low. This was the price of winning, and it made the matches infinitely exciting to watch, with more sub-bogey scores from the two than most would see over a full month's play. Championship players were often down in four, occasionally even in three, but a two required, as Gille-Copain said, divine intervention.

The players enjoyed a camaraderie comparable to the esprit de corps of King James's elite guard, but their relationships also included a healthy undercurrent of competitiveness and resentment that once in a while, as with siblings, would erupt into sharp stares and the occasional barbed comment. All was not jolly, but while they couldn't conceal their identities, they were skilled at concealing their rifts.

Moreover, honor had been woven through the fabric of the competition, which in turn offered more opportunities to display it than any other pastime or, for that matter, society itself. Golf was in this respect a heightened version of everyday existence. Honor might be demonstrated more easily in this medium, but when people recognized it in a player, they assumed this was part of what defined him. And the players, knowing they were revered, worked hard to uphold their image. This entire convention raised everyone's level of awareness. Golf was not simply a matter of getting a ball in a hole. Players knew that by making a spectacle of themselves they risked becoming villains to the galleries, and no one wanted that. If their gentlemanly demeanor in many cases began as a ruse because it was expected, over the course of many years and matches this, along with their individual understanding of how fickle victory was at high levels, brought them together as truly honorable brethren. In later life, long past competition, they were often inseparable friends, regardless of station.

On many occasions, appreciation for the public was the last thing players learned as they fought their way into elite competition; many spoke privately of how poorly the rank and file played or even understood the game. But any overt ill will was frowned upon because the players knew instinctively that they needed the galleries to achieve and maintain their fame, not to mention the welfare of the game.

There were perhaps a dozen or so players in all Scotland who could compete at the highest level, but only eight made it to the finals of the St. Andrews championship on a regular basis, with few changes each year. There was an even smaller group of regular winners who were the *favorites.* A few would age and fall behind, replaced by some new phenomenon or dogged journeyman, and this was always big news. Except for one newcomer, the final eight in 1457 were all familiar faces.

The Dandy

The eldest of the active group was Mal-Giric Alexander from Perth, a dandy who was legendary for devouring life both in daylight on the links and after dark on the town. He was always dressed to the nines, like an earl, and often showed up for matches in a splendid carriage, still dressed for his festivities of the previous night. He was not an earl but, in fact, as close to a professional as there was at the time. A friendly, daring and commanding player, spectacular in both talent and style, he actually was able to make his living from the game as a much sought-after playing partner for nobility and local officials throughout the realm, ensuring his fame the previous decade by contending every year and winning the championship twice. In 1457 he was still a grand emissary, though his star was being eclipsed by brilliant up-and-comers, not to mention a case of whisky fingers.

The Blacksmith

Mal-Giric's competition on this day was a stone of a man named Adam Paternis, a blacksmith and, at every event, the common man's favorite. He eventually would be credited with bringing great hordes out onto the links to see him play, wildly and boldly, charging on every hole, often overpowering his opponent not only with his slashing and heroic swing but also by the vociferousness of his gallery, and despite its considerable size he seemed conversant with each and every one of them. Most believed they too could be like Adam, so they'd scrimp for weeks to buy or barter for clubs and a single ball with which to try their luck, hopefully hacking away. The vast majority silently understood they were *not* Adam but, just as quietly, *imagined* they were. He was at once their leader, hero and teacher, so at even the smallest local competition they would swarm after him like an army, whooping and hollering after his every fearless slash.

With powerful forearms, massive hands and a V-shaped back, he was as physically imposing as a mighty statue, and fleeting expressions of utmost joy or agony played over his great chiseled face. Adam Paternis was the idol of men and the secret dream of women. Given his friendliness and his uncanny knack for remembering names, he was easy prey for any excited fool who was desperate to describe his own banal and hopeless adventures on the links, but Adam would nonetheless listen genuinely to even the worst bore and encourage him to continue practicing, strive always to get better and, above all, never give up.

Adam also enjoyed great success as a blacksmith, following in his father's footsteps, and he used this skill to make his own golf clubs, some of the most imaginative to date. In fact, he also made clubs for other regional competitors, joking that he might just as well be forging swords for his enemies. But he was a man of immense spirit and simply loved club making and championship play—the heart of the game. He fashioned a driving club out of iron rather than wood because wooden play-clubs were apt to break when subjected to the highly percussive impact of elite players; the face of his metal play-club was so thin it was said to be a spring, shooting the ball off at great speed. Adam's strength enabled him to swing clubs freely that most players would find too heavy, and this unique weapon proved so effective in his hands that it soon became known as the Queen's Cannon, after the wife of King James II, Mary of Gueldres, who'd brought eight newly cast cannon from Flanders as a part of her dowry.

In fact, for the most foolish of reasons, the United Golf Honours Society took Adam to task, arguing that this play-club provided an unfair advantage. But he also made them for others, as he pointed out in the heat of the discussions, and then stated for the record that what he really wanted was for the average golfer to have a good time. Nothing ever came of this, not officially. The ruling body, despite its exclusively highborn membership, wilted in the face of Adam's huge, nearly universal appeal and the fact that he cared only for the good of the game. In the end, this was just a club. It had a metal head, as did others, with the same springy hickory shaft and soft leather grip. It wasn't the *club* that allowed Adam to power the ball so far down the fair ways, it was *Adam*.

In the first match—on Sunday, February 20, in a howling wind—Adam beat Mal-Giric Alexander, who showed up as usual at the last minute and saw his play-club desert him, possibly because he was in awe of the Queen's Cannon. It was over after six holes, with Alexander three down when they returned from across the dune behind the wind.

The Wee Ice Mon

THE NEXT quarterfinal match that day was between Nectan MacGregor and Baithin Douglas. Baithin had enjoyed a solid early career but nearly lost his life in a gruesome carriage accident. He wasn't expected to survive or, when he did, to be able to walk, much less play golf. But he battled back, to the amazement of all, and seemingly willed his way to health and competition, returning to the game with the mind of a seasoned veteran but the body of a man learning physical skills all over again. Through interminable practice and indomitable will, the power of the mind overrode the frailties of the body. He learned his true strengths and limitations, and rigorous discipline brought him to play in seven championships and win five, a record.

Baithin Douglas was quiet, many thought surly. As such, even his followers regarded him more as an ideal than a friend. He was alone on the links and shared his life with precious few others. In fact, he became known as the Wee Ice

Mon, a playing machine, an incessant practicer and completely focused competitor. His unrivaled consistency gave his opponents every opportunity to make errors. A superb shot maker before his tragic accident, he was nothing less than legendary afterward.

His dark demeanor was not lost on the Scots, who in his steely expression saw their own truest self. They knew he was agonizing or exulting and fixed their gaze on him, but there was never any outward sign. He spoke little and played brilliantly—colorful in his lack of color, a special and essential piece of the mosaic.

The Blond

Douglas's opponent was the almost mythical Nectan MacGregor, a three-time champion who'd been runner-up the year before. A thousand years earlier, his ancestors had come from the Rhine river valley to Scotland—or Alba, as it was known to the Romans—and settled in a village called Berwick south of the Firth of Forth. Nectan had beaten all comers since he was eleven, mostly because he was able even at that tender age to launch the ball prodigious distances; he reached the longest of holes in two shots, and on the fair greens he literally willed the ball into the hole. Slightly taller than most, he had the cherubic good looks of a big farm boy, with powerful legs and an almost chunky waistline but surprisingly small hands. He also had sloping shoulders, and his neck protruded forward as much as upward, especially when he addressed the ball, but his hallmark was a full head of very fine blond hair and bright blue eyes. He'd become well known for a number of reasons, first and foremost because he was magnificently powerful. Second, he was now in his early thirties, a seasoned veteran of the wars in the links; though his family operated an apothecary, his attention focused mostly on the yearly competitions. Like Mal-Giric Alexander, he often partnered with the higher classes and reaped rich rewards, seldom risking personal loss because he was backed by sponsors. From the age of eleven, his lot in life had been fixed.

Unquestionably athletic, he was not fast afoot but strong. His powers of concentration were exceptional, and in the heat of battle, when he needed a shot or a putt, he made it. Everyone could tell when one of these master strokes was about to occur, because his forehead would contort into one continuous blond eyebrow, and below that his blue eyes were so bright they could bore holes into granite. His demeanor in competition, especially in his younger days, was nearly mean-spirited, with a focus so intense that he seemed determined to defeat his opponent not only tactically but emotionally. But after the passing of his beloved father, who'd been instrumental in his success, and at the urging of a handful of elders and competitive friends, he softened his image. After a solid decade of dominance, he found he didn't need to be so grimly offensive. This launched him into a new era, and now he was regarded as one of the rulers of the game.

Blessed with an incredible memory, Nectan could recall every shot he'd ever hit in competition, as well as minutiae from myriad conversations, and he often would summon up such items, which made him appear even more intelligent. He became expert on a variety of subjects; behind his back, and in fun, other competitors punningly referred to him as "Fourth," not because he had to cross the Firth of Forth en route to most events but because he conducted himself as if he were a fourth wise man.

His only unimpressive feature was a tiny high-pitched

speaking voice, a comical anomaly in an otherwise commanding presence.

He was, without question, more completely focused than anyone else when engaged on the links. When Nectan stood over the ball with his head sticking straight out from his chest, he was the picture of athletic power. At address, he never allowed his play-club to touch or rest on the turf, and he placed the ball high atop a pinch of damp sand from deep within the hole. "Air," he would say, "resists less than dirt." Then, after what seemed an eternity, his head would turn slightly to the right and his hands would *push* the club straight back from the ball to the top of the swing, where the shaft would be perfectly aligned with the target and level with the ground. The force with which the clubhead met the ball was astonishing.

Nectan MacGregor, of course, had been expected to reach the finals, but Baithin Douglas made eight consecutive fours against him in the bitter wind. Naturally, both men were cold and intermittent rain hounded them, especially once they headed over the dune on the third and fourth holes. Nectan stayed close, losing the second, winning the fifth and seventh and then sinking a twenty-footer to halve and win the match at the final fair green, leaving everyone but Baithin visibly excited.

The Highlander

The third match featured Samsone MacLeod and Colaim Cummings. MacLeod had come a long way to compete in Fife. He was a Highland shepherd from Applecross Forest in Ross Cromarty on the west coast of Scotland, an affable soul whose natural talent perhaps surpassed that of any other active player. But he was also a fierce competitor, with a golf swing so amazingly graceful and fluid that it was known throughout the land.

Samsone made a fair amount of money taking on all comers and spotting them strokes on each hole to egg them on. Occasionally he came away the loser, but these matches did more to forge him as a competitor than any amount of practice. He was also blessed with a marvelous sense of humor, which masked his deadly competitiveness to all but his opponents, who knew to expect subtle shenanigans from this colorful character. "Aye, it's glad I am not to have *that* shot," he'd say quietly, as an opponent studied a particularly difficult situation—a comment that could be devastating to an unsuspecting newcomer, causing him to wonder if he was facing some unnoticed disaster. As the better younger players got to know him, they sometimes would give it right back, and when they did he only laughed. Samsone's greatest fame, however, derived from the fact that despite his peerless natural talent and more victories in regular competition than any other player, Samsone MacLeod had *never* won a championship.

The Natural

MacLeod's competition that day was an old friend from a town in the far south, Whithorn, the birthplace of Ninian, Scotland's first resident saint, allowing, of course, that Andrew wasn't a Scot. More than a thousand years later, Whithorn brought forth another luminary in the only son of Clara and Colaim Cummings the Elder, a successful barrister known for defending the poor and heaping righteous indignation upon the greedy in the small courts of the region. He was as colorful as he was effective, often citing such ancient legends of saints, as Ninian, Columba or his favorite, St. Mungo, meaning "very dear one" in Gaelic. Many times he recounted the tale of a feudal king who refused to support the church. Mungo called a curse down on the king, which brought forth a devastating rainstorm, the River Clyde conveniently overflowing through the king's grain barns and sweeping its stores downriver to Mungo's feet, where they were distributed to the poor. Greed would be overcome by righteousness, and Colaim the Elder justly popular.

Colaim the Younger came into the world a rather sickly boy, very much in his father's shadow and always aware that his conduct would be judged accordingly. They often played golf together, after one of his father's friends gave him a cut-down club and several balls; it became his passion. Like his father, he went on to study law at St. Andrews University and spent many hours on those links, befriended by the shepherds and proving remarkably adept at and deeply committed to the game. But perhaps because he was accustomed to success in his youth, failures on the links seemed incomprehensible and caused him, from time to time, to forget his upbringing, a youthful weakness. He rarely lost his temper, but when he did it was Vesuvian. The classic natural, he was handsome, gifted at everything he attempted and, in his eventual prime on the links, a powerful, unstoppable force. Colaim began winning major events at an early age and was the very model of honorable conduct, save for his eruptions. His parents' chastisements unfortunately, as is often the case, had little effect, but within a few years a young lady named Mary made it clear she wouldn't have anything to do with a hothead, and walked away. Crushed, Colaim finally realized that his tantrums were a liability both on and off the links. Losing this girl felt like a mortal blow, though true to form he didn't give up.

As soon as he could, he scheduled another contest with a worthy competitor and begged Mary to attend.

There were dozens in the gallery that day, even though it was only a friendly match. Talent in this burgeoning age of golf was so appreciated that Colaim Cummings always drew a crowd, and while he would never admit to it, he threw the match in order to demonstrate his new persona and remained gracious to a fault.

His opponent pulled him aside afterward and said, " 'Fess up, Colaim. What's goin' on? Ye dinna seem yourself. That odd shot ye hit into the last hole was like ye'd aimed for the whins."

Colaim just looked at him, smiling, and then, impishly, he winked. "Later," he said.

But his scheme had given him an inadvertent whiff of sportsmanship. With his anger under control, he'd been able to appreciate what it meant to lose graciously, and this was far more satisfying than any fit of pique. The lesson he taught himself that day would identify him for the remainder of his life. As to losing like a gentleman—well, he had few occasions to practice, winning as he did far more often than he lost.

Colaim conquered himself first and then his competitors. He also matured into a burgeoning young barrister, assisting his father for a number of years before striking out on his own. With his new wife—Mary, wouldn't you know?—he moved to Perth, where he apprenticed himself to a parliamentarian and then to a high-ranking officer in the Justiciary, the department of justice. He'd found his vocation but never forsook his avocation. In fact, his prowess on the links was paramount in his appointments, and his remarkable ability as a player encapsulated his other talents. He was a special person and—hands down—the greatest player alive for a considerable period.

One year, in his absolute prime, he won the four biggest events—a feat never accomplished by any other player. The heart of his game was scrappiness, an absolute refusal to concede defeat. His credo, once he'd gained control of his emotions, was that he owed his opponent nothing less than his very best, and this made defeating him an even greater accomplishment.

Well-born gentleman, man of letters, he nonetheless showed not a trace of condescension; his respect for fellow competitors was both obvious and sincere. But by 1457, he was also among the oldest players and had recently been complaining to Mary of pain in his legs.

His match that day looked as though the sweet swinging MacLeod would polish him off in a hurry, while the skies darkened and a nasty slashing rain made every shot dangerous. Still, as long as the ball didn't blow off the fair green, play would continue. After losing the first four holes, Cummings won the next four. Then, downwind on the first extra hole, MacLeod hit a colossal drive through the fair way into an irrecoverable lie and his undoing. A typical win for Colaim, perhaps, in coming back from disaster, but it left MacLeod shaking his head in discouragement.

Baggage

As irony would have it, John Brighte, in another quarterfinal match against Caeril Patersone, relied on his short game to keep him alive, much as it had the year before. His deftness in the fringes was hardly what brought out his massive galleries, however. No one could hit the ball farther, and Brighte's power never failed to amaze them.

He was dogged by tragedy, and assuaged it in the taverns.

His binges were epic, appalling, pitiful and expected. Still, he played incredibly well while carrying this heavy baggage. Lacking both the charisma of Paternis and the style of Alexander, he became known for this failing and finally admitted to it, and, not surprisingly, public sentiment swung in his favor, possibly because a great many people faced the same challenge. John tried to straighten up, yet failed time after time. Even so, the emotion that coursed through his gallery was pure interminable hope. Because of his honesty as much as his majestic game, they wanted John Brighte to succeed and in this way, perhaps, escape his demons.

The Newcomer

Caeril Patersone was finally in; his dream had at last come true, and in this changing age he and Samsone MacLeod were the only shepherds in the final eight. Tall, rangy and handsome, he had a brilliant smile and a graceful swing. He was also as friendly as Colaim Cummings, as powerful as Nectan MacGregor and potentially as charismatic as Adam Paternis. Moreover, Caeril was just twenty, a good six years younger than Brighte and at least a decade younger than anyone else in the field.

Gille-Copain had been right about the inevitability of Caeril's arrival at championship level. He'd beaten nearly everyone he faced for three straight years running, with the exception of John Brighte, though he'd finally overcome that obstacle, beating him head-to-head at Anstruther the previous fall.

John's prodigious opening drive would have dismantled any player's concentration—except Caeril's. As John walked away from the shot, expecting Caeril's wide-eyed response, he saw only a slightly quizzical stare and the hint of a grin on Caeril's and Micael's faces. John's desired effect backfired; it was he who became confused, hit a poor approach and lost the opening hole to Caeril's brilliant mid-iron to within a foot. It was all downhill from there. Caeril won three of the first four holes, halved the next and won the match by actually outdriving John at six, and halving the hole for the win, 3 and 2.

THIS SET THE STAGE for the semifinals, to be held the following Sunday, the last Sunday of February. Nectan MacGregor would play Colaim Cummings, and Caeril Patersone would face Adam Paternis. Followers of the vanquished were as disappointed as their players, but everyone would return to watch the semifinals. Gille-Copain would again hold court in Tippin's, furthering the magic as the competitive year built to a crescendo.

Clubmen and Rulers

AT THE ELITE LEVEL, the players were not alone. Each would have an assistant, or a clubman, not yet known as a caddie. (That term first referred to the sons of French nobility, *cadets,* who served as pages for Mary, Queen of Scots, but Mary would not appear in Scotland for another sixty years, and eventually *caddie* referred to Edinburgh street people who ran errands for money.) In 1457, the players' assistants were mere clubmen, and many were entertaining, colorful and, in some cases, maddening.

The idea took shape around 1270 during Scotland's Golden Era, when nobility and the wealthy discovered that the game was highly appealing. But as with everything else, they had to put their own twist on it. Many assembled huge selections of clubs to address every possible occurrence on the links and this soon became more than an armful, so the well-to-do quickly determined that a carriage boy or house servant should lug them around while they grandly strutted the few meager yards between swings, where the comedy would be reenacted. For commoners, this ludicrous affectation was a great source of hilarity.

But the participation of the privileged added credibility to the game. Even kings had staff bring them clubs and balls to be examined, perhaps with rug shots caroming off the paintings of namesakes over the fireplace while courtiers dove for cover. But it would not be until the mid-sixteenth century before Mary, Queen of Scots, ventured onto the links to mix it up with the Great Unwashed.

Hard-core clubmen then were much as they are now, a catch-as-catch-can group of children, seniors and miscreants. The clubman never changed. He learned the game, played some and bet on anything at all, from a frog race to whether a player would make a one-foot putt. In general, everyday clubmen knew a great deal about the game but had little respect for themselves or for life in general. They almost always had good sense about breaks on fair greens or what shots were possible. Still, being a full-time clubman was considered to be the end of the road, though some had as much style as the players for whom they labored. As a rule, clubmen were either old men or young boys. The former were a crusty bunch and usually the reason mothers wouldn't allow their sons to follow in their footsteps.

Nectan MacGregor recounted his experiences with clubmen in the cathedral close following his victory in 1451, when asked the difference between the wild-haired Alphonso MacPhee, who had carried for him in this event, and Wee Willie Ogilvie, whom he'd used in two previous successful championships.

"Well," he said, "Alphonso paced off every distance and come to me with eighty-three over the sand in front and eleven steps to the hole, leavin' me with the math, and then he's tellin' me about the wind that's knockin' us over, pitchin' a bit of grass and watchin' it disappear sideways. And then he's tellin' me about the stance and how the fair green's fallin' away, and waitin' for me to tell him the club, though we're both knowin' full well which.

"But Willie? Ah, Wee Willie. No ceremony with him. He just hands me the mid-iron and says, 'Go git 'em, laddie.' "

But a clubman is effective in lending assistance to even the worst player, more often than not being far better at the game. Even so, his player might complain about having "the worst clubman in the world!" To which the clubman would answer, "I think not, sir, that would be too great a coincidence."

Or the player could ask, "Do ye think I can get home with the mid-iron?" Exasperated, the clubman might hand him the club and mutter, "Aye, *eventually.*"

But when the player was superb, the clubman would rise to the occasion and do many things beyond carrying the equipment. (There were no golf bags in those days, only an armful of clubs, an extra ball or two in a pouch or pocket, and perhaps a rag to clean them.) Under pressure of competition, the clubman could be invaluable. He would be out in the fair way to be sure he could find his player's incoming ball; when a match depended on the subtleties of a fair green, it was very reassuring to have another set of eyes to confirm the break or the speed.

And every once in a while, clubman and player would be friends, and their conversations were more than the game. Such was the case with Caeril Patersone and Micael Carrick. The mutual admiration that had brought them together had kept them together. By now both knew their lot in life had been set, each of them committed to continue furthering their mastery. The only significant difference between them, and this they discussed many times over the years, was that Caeril's existence dealt with the preservation of his flock, whereas Micael's was antithetical. Hardened by exposure to hunting almost from infancy, Micael knew what it was to bring down a deer and put it quickly out of its misery by slitting its throat. Both boys understood this, but for Caeril the act of cutting was very painful. The shot from the bow was part of a game, and he always prayed the arrow would finish the job; the alternative was nearly unthinkable.

"The knife's easy for ye, Micael," he said.

His friend shrugged. "It's right that the beast not suffer. And ye know we must eat and have warm clothes."

This conversation moved through other versions of killing and whether or not, if called to war like their fathers, either could kill a man.

"If it was me or him," Caeril said, "aye. But I'm *not* sure about doin' it from a distance. Could ye do it?"

With little hesitation and less emotion, Micael's answer was simple, just a familiar nod of the head and twist of the mouth. There was no question.

Micael Carrick would become a primary force in the strife of the days to come.

As always, where there is success or excitement, there are also those who, by virtue of station, frivolously insert themselves. Such was the case with the United Golf Honours Society, which had evolved out of regional organizations over two decades before, in what was itself a battle royal. Generally, it was run by golf novices who enjoyed having authority, and since golf was regarded as the shepherds' game, the society's logic was simple: Shepherds must be regulated, supervised, controlled. Again, by virtue of their station, it was easy for those men to assume command. But because they understood only the *letter* of the rules and had never experienced them firsthand in high levels of competition, the players who lived and died by those rules found it difficult to accept their authority. They had always honored the rules unswervingly and were expert in their interpretation of them. Offenders were quickly extricated, before any official ever heard about it. However, the society insisted that without them there would *be* no game. In their minds, the United Golf Honours Society *was* the game, and this the players deeply resented.

The society ratified its position of prominence simply by showing up and naming events as they saw fit. They claimed to oversee the development of the ball, the clubs and the links, but in fact they had no real expertise and very little control over any of these things. They brought in other amateurs and wealthy dilettantes who claimed expertise simply because they were slightly better-than-average players themselves and could provide incomprehensible data to support whatever crusade was deemed relevant by the appointed head of the society, who performed his duties with relentless pomp.

The players could only roll their eyes. They knew the rules because they used them at every turn. In fact, at the end of the day, the rules *belonged* to them and they would frequently, especially in the late-winter matches, discuss changes or actually make them. The United Golf Honours Society would listen and then spread the word as if it had been their decision.

The notion of regulating equipment was also meaningless. Along with the players' abilities, the clubs and especially balls constantly improved, which in turn called for longer holes. A hue and cry frequently rose up to demand that the new equipment should be banned or else the *real game* would fade from existence. But the gallery loved power. People wanted to see colossal drives and deft play from the fair ways. The game had developed into a quest for length. The players sought it, the people marveled at it and even the United Golf Honours Society knew it was crucial, so its restriction was moot. All holes eventually became too short. Older two-shot holes were routinely reached in one by the likes of MacGregor, Cummings, Patersone and Paternis, and in length Brighte was perhaps in a class by himself.

The crowds were a factor as well. Players were ranked variously, by gentry, by station, by trade and especially by region, but a general din constantly proclaimed that certain players would prevail over others. Moreover, people chose their favorites based on the past, not the pulse of the moment, and rarely could tell who was striking the ball particularly well. In truth, the field was very closely matched. Still, many were convinced that, in 1457, Nectan would beat Colaim and Adam would beat Caeril and then Nectan, for some inexplicable reason, would beat Adam.

The players enjoyed the adulation and were fiercely competitive, but there was a cancer rampant in the game that was beyond anyone's control, possibly excepting James II himself. Betting was both epidemic and overt, and the advent of coins made it that much easier. Even sharp reprimands from the pulpit didn't ease the problem. There were bets placed on every match, and the usual beatings when an overzealous believer wagered more than he could possibly afford to pay. But by and large, the bets were small, friendly and without incident—except in one monumental case.

Skullduggery

THE SMALL SOD-ROOF farmhouse sat in a shadowy little glade. Built in the thirteenth century, it had stayed in the same family ever since. They had come from the county of Ayr in the southwest when trouble erupted between Sir William Wallace and the English sheriff of Lanark. The family head, Barton, felt that Fife would be much safer, with the expansive Firth of Forth to provide a barrier to any warring factions moving north.

Settling in this small inland cove, he became known around Boarhills as Barton of Ayr and, soon, just Barton Ayr. Early in the fourteenth century, a local chieftain married one of the Ayr daughters, reported to have been ravishingly beautiful, and she bore him a gaggle of bright, beautiful children. In gratitude, and in testimony to her beauty and grace, he converted her family's farm to freehold status. No longer were the Ayrs serfs; they now *owned* this tiny kingdom south of St. Andrews. Generation after generation farmed the land, eventually raising cattle.

Legend held that a swine cult had flourished here before

the birth of Christ, presumably due to the prevalence of wild boars, but over the course of time pigs were introduced, though they have never been significant in Scottish agriculture. Nonetheless, the Ayr homestead was known as the Pig Farm, located at the end of the ancient New Pig Lane, despite the complete absence of these animals. For almost two centuries the family had prospered here, for as freeholders they were only occasionally subject to the shenanigans of various feudal lords and kings. The generation now occupying the farm was Morgunn Ayr and his wife, Olandra, whose daughter, Eta, was a sterling representation of her legendary ancestor, a feisty and breathtakingly beautiful young woman of eighteen years.

The countryside sported a flamboyant character, a noble named Ruadri Townsend. It was not known whether his problems arose from having too many things or not enough love or just a shortfall of intelligence; whatever the cause, his life was a succession of crises. He had survived various attacks on his honor, although his behavior did not reflect well on his highly regarded father. Fortunately for him, he was one of those people who, when stepping into a mess, appeared to be dancing; he was as adept as a toreador at sidestepping trouble and moved unmarried on to middle age, avoiding one disaster after another. When his father died, he was left as the only child with a considerable family fortune. While maintaining the family seat in St. Andrews, he took his father's seat in Parliament at Perth. Of course his parents had many very convenient friends. One of them, William Dobarchon, was a brilliant financier, unrivaled in his time; another friend was none other than Bishop James Kennedy.

Mordiac Domni was a lender who awoke every day wondering what duties he would perform in the oiling of his great money machine. He had received an exceptional education in his long affiliation with William Dobarchon, who combined financial acumen and civic responsibility. Since Dobarchon and his lovely wife, Blaire, never had children, Mordiac became their surrogate son and learned his trade first as apprentice, then as clerk, and finally as partner. In boyhood, he had become Ruadri Townsend's closest friend—both of them lucky children who would prove untrustworthy.

William and Blaire followed the doctrines of the Romanized church and trained Mordiac accordingly. Rather than simply line his pockets, Dobarchon operated his money-lending institution almost as a charity, offering loans to those in need and coaching them toward solvency. An astute businessman, he was an even better inspirational teacher. With more than enough to satisfy his own needs, he wanted everyone in greater St. Andrews to be financially self-sufficient, and he also contributed generously to the church. Because of his efforts, many hard-pressed citizens came to understand money better and treat it not as an end in itself but as the means to a greater good.

No one took more from his lessons than Mordiac, who absorbed every detail of Dobarchon's business, and did not let greed become his opiate until he was made partner. William, believing that Mordiac had a similarly gracious nature, wanted him to inherit the business, and Mordiac was a very good actor indeed. Long before inheritance was an issue, he began skimming a little here and a little there. Then, when William became preoccupied with Blaire's failing health, he upped the ante, reveling in his ability to pit one entity unknowingly against another; as one prevailed, the other became his property. He managed to hide all this from his mentor; when first Blaire and then William died, Mordiac saw to it that they received nearly regal funerals, the entire community lining up to pay their respects to a man from whom they'd learned so much, not only about money but also about considering and caring for others.

Unfortunately, Mordiac was silently maturing into a bastard of the first order. And his closest boyhood friend, Sir Ruadri Townsend, had a problem that would lead the countryside into legend and the game of golf into immortality.

THE MORNING AFTER the quarterfinals, Mordiac Domni was greasing yet another cog in his money machine. He dismounted at the house at the end of New Pig Lane and tied the reins to a post. The door was already open, and he was greeted quizzically by Olandra Ayr, who on the best of days was merely tolerant of Domni. His visit today alarmed her. Was there some problem with the loan they'd secured two years earlier? Surely this rotund ugly dwarf couldn't be here to court Eta?

Eta *was* primary in Domni's thoughts, though for a completely different reason. Like her forebears, she had shining black hair, bright blue eyes and a quick wit; in fact, the entire family was smart, as Mordiac would discover. Nevertheless, two years earlier he'd managed to persuade Morgunn that borrowing money to expand the farm's facilities would help increase his revenues. What the Ayrs didn't know was that he had already loaned money on the same premise to the area's only butcher, or flesher. Six months later, and just before slaughter, Domni convinced other crofters from Leuchars and farther to the west toward Cupar to take their cattle to the flesher south of St. Andrews, since their only local flesher had recently died somewhat mysteriously. This was Domni's good luck but bad news for Morgunn, whose flesher was now too busy to handle his animals. Domni had advised each of them not to discuss their loans with anyone, especially those with whom they did business. This turn of events forced Morgunn to slaughter the cattle himself, but his profits suffered because most meat was purchased by the upper classes, and exclusively from established butchers.

Domni had set his trap with cold calculation, allowing the fleshers to convert one loan while arranging for the Ayrs' loan to fail. His goal wasn't Eta at all but the farm.

On this day, however, he was developing another scheme, this one with the Ayrs' full knowledge. His idea was to use Eta to distract Caeril, causing him to lose his match with Adam, whom Domni's friend Townsend was convinced would subsequently lose to MacGregor, on whom he'd placed a huge wager. Domni knew neither Caeril nor Eta was attached and might find each other attractive. Morgunn should be receptive to his idea, he thought, since Domni would reduce his financial obligation if Eta cooperated.

Olandra was fearful of the shadow Mordiac Domni had cast over their lives. She was civil, though, and invited him for sweetbread, which he refused.

Before long, Morgunn, who'd seen Domni ride up, came in, shook his hand and sat down at the table, eyeing him with suspicion and concern. Domni had been on the farm only once before, for the signing of the loan agreement that had allowed Morgunn to expand the barn and yard with new stalls for additional livestock. It had seemed like a happy day back then. Everyone, especially the lender, had been smiling.

But now, with the fleshing issue still unresolved and his revenues dwindling, Morgunn was disheartened. In fact, running more cattle had actually drained his resources, and he found himself having to cut exorbitant amounts of hay, forcing Olandra and Eta into the fields. This had been going on for over a year, and though no repayments had been missed, the family was hovering very near the financial edge.

"So what brings ye back here, then?" Morgunn asked.

"I've an idea that could be to yer best interest," Domni said, cutting his eyes sharply toward him but not meeting his gaze.

"I'll listen, sure, things not havin' gone as well as I'd hoped."

"Aye, it's been hard times here on the coast, but you seem to be stayin' current."

"Current's a matter of sweat," Morgunn told him. "The spring hay'll be welcome, for we're travelin' too far to cut silage. The animals, they're testin' our limits. If I could just sell the flesher a few more cows, it would ease the strain."

"He's to his limit, as I understand," Domni said. He had instructed the flesher to send an apprentice to the Ayrs every two months to take only one animal, while at the same time suggesting this was all Morgunn wanted to sell. Mistakenly, both men trusted Domni, chiefly because William Dobarchon had been so forthright, and his adopted son had converted their trust into the collateral he so fervently desired. When the time was right, Mordiac would pull a string, the flesher would refuse to buy Morgunn's cows and Morgunn wouldn't be able to hold on. Mordiac would then foreclose on this perfectly good farm and return the Ayrs to serfdom.

"Strange, ain't it? That he canna take my animals?"

"It'll not likely do any good, but let me have another word with him. Don't speak to him yerself, though. It's not to your advantage, lettin' him know ye need him. But now, my friend, I've come across an idea ye might like. Can we walk and talk?"

Morgunn studied the little man, puzzled that he should invoke friendship. "Aye," he said, and rose from the benches. Olandra still eyed this visitor with disdain and walked out the door to the lane.

"I'm concerned about yer production," Domni began, "and can see ye're struggling to keep up with the animals. But extensions are difficult to justify. I, too, am feelin' pressured. Things are slow, ye know?"

"Don't want an extension," Morgunn snapped. "Determined I am to ride this out."

"Well . . ." Domni paused, wishing the farmer was a little more desperate. "I've an idea that would maybe ease the pressure."

"Which idea is that?"

"I'll make it plain, Morgunn. I've noted, as has the entire town, that Eta has become a beautiful woman."

Glowering, Morgunn stepped in front of the much smaller Domni. "What has any of this to do with Eta?" he asked sternly.

"Please! Hear me out."

"Eta's my only child, *friend,* and at the moment I need her."

"I'm not proposin' to take her away," Domni was quick to say. "I only need—uh, well, her attributes."

"Attributes?"

"Consider what I'd like Eta to do as only a bit of a game, but I am willin' to compensate ye for it."

Morgunn stared at him darkly. "And what is it she's to do? Yer words fall heavy on my ears."

"Eta is unattached," Domni said, in a matter-of-fact tone, "and it appears suitors are reluctant to approach because—well, she's nearly *too* bonny."

"Aye, it's the truth, that. But then so was her mother. And?"

"Well, I'd like Eta to strike up a relationship, ye might say, or at least to allow it."

"Whatever for? Why? What are ye goin' on about?"

"Morgunn, it's harmless *fun.* She has but to make the acquaintance of a lad. What she does with it is her business."

"A lad? And what lad might he be?"

"He's called Caeril Patersone."

"Patersone? The *shepherd* Patersone?"

"Aye, he's a shepherd."

Morgunn's eyebrows furrowed, and the corners of his mouth turned downward. "Eta's nae strikin' up with any shepherd! Why should she? What is the purpose of this madness?" His voice had risen so sharply that Olandra glanced out the window.

"What else, then, do ye know of the lad?"

"Not a bloody thing. That he's a shepherd is quite enough."

"Whereas ye raise cattle so what's the grave difference?"

"We *both* know the difference."

"Nae, that's just perception. Do ye know what he really is?"

Silence.

"The lad's a champion golfer."

"As all shepherds are, I'm sure."

"Hear me, Morgunn. Caeril Patersone is a *champion.* Few if any can beat him."

"I know nothin' of the golf. I'm too busy feedin' my beasts."

"Perhaps not, but this lad holds the key to a box of gold, and ye might could share in *that.*" Domni winced, knowing that he'd overstated the case.

"And how's that?" Morgunn said slyly.

"Well, he beat one of the greats Sunday last, John Brighte."

"Brighte! That farmer from Crail? *Him* I've heard of."

"Aye, he did."

"He *must* be good, then. But what this has to do with Eta is a mystery still."

"There's another match come Sunday, the next round. Patersone plays Paternis."

"Paternis? Now *that* one's famous, he is!"

"Aye. They say he's the king of golf."

"And?" Morgunn asked, forcing the point.

"Patersone canna win."

"Sure, it's no way he could win against the Queen's Cannon." Now Morgunn had completely given himself away, but Domni was too busy scheming to notice.

"Many would beg to differ. Patersone's young and strong, and he beat Brighte, the only man who hits it farther than Paternis. There's much gold ridin' on the match. Some—uh, very *influential* people expect Paternis to win. If he doesn't, aye, it's problems all round. The game has fixed everyone's attention."

Morgunn sensed an advantage. "A bet, eh? Or is it *your* attention and *your* money?"

"*I* have nae money for gamblin'," Domni retorted, "and I don't play at golf. But I have been approached by someone—well, in government—who's worryin' that some folks are over-extended with the betting."

"Government?"

"Well, Morgunn, the crux is your Eta is bonny enough to distract the lad, and at that level it wouldna take much for him to lose, maybe only one shot. One shot could be the match!"

"Mordiac," Morgunn said thoughtfully, "I dunna see how distractin' some golfer can cure the problems of the realm."

"What?" Domni fumbled, realizing how badly he'd allowed his pitch to stray. "Well, if we destroy the sure thing, people will be less apt to bet, do ye not think?"

Morgunn rubbed his beard, placed his hand on the back of his neck and spoke into the ground. "Nae."

"What?"

"Nae," Morgunn said quietly.

"You're nay-saying the plan? But it's *easy!*"

"Nae. Dunna want Eta in this scheme. Doubt she'd do it anyway."

Domni was silent, his eyes darting back and forth between Morgunn, the ground and the house. The only other solution would be to *kill* Patersone, and he wanted nothing to do with that. "Of course," he said, "if times dunna improve, ye will fall behind for sure. It would be a great shame, that."

The discussion was becoming distasteful, and Morgunn knew he had to show Domni he was ready to stand and fight. "Aye, a shame. But if ye're thinkin' to call in the loan, I'll take that chance because ye canna do it unless I'm in arrears. I'm not likin' this idea, nor any more of yer talk. It's over."

Now in disarray, Domni moved toward his mount, but then turned back with a contrite demeanor.

"I dunna understand your objection," he said.

"Eta's reputation is pure. Canna ask her to risk otherwise, wouldna ask," Morgunn replied. "This is nae a national problem, just some rich man's mistake."

"Aye, Morgunn, but everything has its price, does it not, Ayr? And besides, ye can help the country too."

"The *country*? Ha! Patersone's not King Henry, attackin'

our fair land, he's a golfin' shepherd, for all that's holy! If I'm to convince my daughter and my wife to do somethin', dunna know what, to distract this lad, I'll need more than patriotic sheep dung for it. I canna say what you have in this, but I expect that if it's government ye're representin', ye'll have to bear the brunt of what our negotiations might produce."

"Negotiations?" Domni said. "Do ye feel, in your position, that ye can actually negotiate?"

Morgunn didn't even pause. "In matters of family, only trust in each other matters. If that means I must forfeit all by refusin', so be it. But I'm current, and ye have no call to abuse me. Besides, I'd want something in return if Eta was to compromise herself in any way. Seems to me," he concluded, "if she succeeded in distractin' this lad and ye become famous with those in government, ye should be willin' to forgive my debt."

"What? Forgive it, you say? Morgunn, this is nae more than a simple prank. A prank! How could a small act be worth so much?"

"Well, Mordiac," Morgunn said softly, "why not let your government friends pay off my note if Eta sways the match by blindin' this young wonder? Unless ye're such a patriot ye'd be willin' to sacrifice yer own money for the good of the country—or should I say for some bureaucrat's gamblin' losses? Perhaps they're yer own—"

"They're *nae* mine," Domni snapped, "as I already told ye." He rubbed his chin. "But ye do make a point. So, what's the price then, really?"

Morgunn was ready. "The least we can do is change the terms, extendin' the payments so they're manageable and reducin' the principal by half."

"I'd have to calculate what that really means, and whether

the others would be willin' to cover my cost. I'm just the messenger, but comin' to you *was* my idea. I believe Eta has the talent for success in this."

"Talent?"

"How else would ye say it? She'd be usin' more than her beauty. She'll need her mind to craft a plan to do—well, whatever it might be," he said weakly.

"True, and all the more reason to increase the value."

Mordiac's disappointment at having been beaten by a crofter was somewhat softened by the notion of extracting a guarantee from Townsend instead of shouldering it himself. And with each party ignorant of the other, he could still do everything in his power to manipulate both ends of the deal. He was already inflating the value of the farm as a hedge, and the dirty secrets he had on Ruadri made him doubly comfortable.

"Well, all right, then," Domni said. "Reduce the terms *and* the principal by twenty percent."

"Forty percent," Morgunn shot back.

"Twenty-five."

"Enough hagglin'. I can go up to fifty percent if ye like, or there's no deal."

"Done, damn ye."

"*And* extend the payments over four years."

"Aye." Domni knew the terms were secondary to the indebtedness. As long as Morgunn owed him money he could somehow wheedle the asset. All he wanted now was to escape without further damage. "But only *after* Patersone loses," he added.

"And what guarantee do I have if he does?"

"My word, friend."

"When we borrowed the money," Morgunn said, "we

signed documents. Why canna we nae have new documents? No offense, but your word dunna suffice."

Domni, though shocked by his statement, spoke as if to a schoolboy. "Because the deal's not done. Patersone has not yet lost. That would be unfair to me!"

"Put it in the agreement too, then, that Patersone must lose."

"Agreed, then. I'll have it drawn up." Domni had no desire to have such items actually recorded, but he could finesse that later while concluding the deal on the spot.

"And I'll discuss it with my family. When do I see ye again?"

"I'll be back before dark tomorrow."

"Time enough for Eta to make a plan before the match?"

"Aye, time's of the essence."

They did not shake hands. Mordiac simply turned for his horse, mounted and looked down at Morgunn. "Tomorrow eve," he said. "Maybe sooner."

"I'll be here regardless, findin' food for my animals."

Mordiac gave a small wave that was less a salute than a dismissal, then turned and rode away. Already figuring how to secure Ruadri's guarantee, he headed there directly.

The Hedge

In St. Andrews, Domni found his noble friend where he'd expected, in a tavern. Fortunately, it was early enough that Townsend was still conversant and, with a bit of food in him, might even be decisive. Since they had every reason not to advertise their friendship, they made their greetings formal and loud enough for the other patrons to hear.

"Ho! Lord Townsend. A pleasant surprise, sir."

"Domni, good to see you. Come, sit. Take an ale with me," he said in his baronial best.

"Actually, I'm in need of repast. Would ye join me for dinner?" Mordiac said, staring so intently that the other man couldn't fail to realize they needed to talk.

"Splendid!" Townsend lied, then whispered, "though I'd choose to *drink* my dinner."

Soon they were seated in a quiet booth at the back of the room by a large window overlooking Murray Park, their table filled with mutton, potatoes, beer and apples. Domni explained his plan in hushed tones, constantly glancing nervously over his shoulder. Townsend had sidestepped reason once again, having based his wager on the fact that MacGregor had defeated Paternis in the finals three times in the past. Also, since young Patersone had beaten Brighte, as Brighte had defeated MacGregor the previous year, he was now convinced that the young shepherd would automatically defeat Paternis, spinning Ruadri into poverty. Therefore, Paternis *had* to win the semifinal. The idea that Paternis might rise up to smite MacGregor never crossed Townsend's irrational and desperate mind. With no particular grasp of the game itself, he could see only its history and immediate past results, not what the future or even the present might deliver. And his gambling habit had overcome him just as surely as the drink that brought him nightly to his knees. He was a miserable caged animal in his close and unholy darkness.

Mordiac Domni, having little interest in the game, was far more interested in turning this dilemma to his own advantage.

"I've decided," he concluded, "that to ensure victory for our man we must deploy a special weapon."

"Weapon? Are we to eliminate somebody? That seems a bit harsh, don't you think?"

Domni spoke quietly, slowly, holding his head in his hands. "Nae, we are not about to *hurt* anyone. Remember, this is a golf match, and if anything goes amiss ye canna collect the winnings."

"Oh, aye. Right. Good thinking. But what weapon, then?" He stared into Mordiac's eyes in utter confusion.

"The fair sex."

"That's quite a weapon." Townsend gave a wry smile. "I've certainly got the wounds to show for it."

Domni shook his head. "We're not talkin' about wounds, just a young lad. Patersone's probably not but twenty, and his niblick's harder than his head."

At this Townsend roared and pounded the table, rattling the plates and spilling some of the drink. "So then what?" he said.

"So: the plan." Domni told him about the Ayr family, implying that Eta was willing to play along because she had her own designs on him. He feared this might sound totally absurd, but it gave him a vicarious thrill and also suggested that he had Morgunn over a barrel. "We've not settled the details," he continued, "but we have a plan, and when it comes off our lad Adam will be the benefactor."

Suddenly Townsend grabbed his collar and pulled him close, his guttural whisper slurring his words. "And what if it doesn't work?"

Domni brushed the offending hand from his garment and snarled, "Just like the old days," remembering how in his disturbed youth this rich nobleman delighted in vandalism and was forever getting caught, requiring his humble apprentice to invent alibis. No, it couldn't have been Ruadri who set that barn on fire, because they were fishing together by the Eden. The Dobarchons took him at his word, and the accusations were always dropped. Over time, Domni had made a career of saving Townsend from ruin, and he continued to support him from a distance in his political affairs, knowing these efforts would be rewarded. But he was growing tired of waiting. "Ye made this mess on your own. Sure, I helped ye back then, and maybe I can help ye now, but I'm sick of carryin' the risk by myself. This time there's a *price.*"

He expected this to provoke another uproar, but Townsend sat slumped there mute, his eyes shifting aimlessly—an indication, Domni thought, of a mind very near self-destruction.

"Price? What price, then?" Townsend finally mumbled.

"It was ye comin' to *me,* remember? I'm not the one who

laid a sack of gold on MacGregor. Nae, ye may be my lot in life, but this time, my friend, there's considerable risk, and it's ye who'll bear it, because it's yer problem, not mine."

Townsend was frowning, looking almost on the verge of tears.

"What *price*?" he said, sounding defeated.

"The only reason Eta would do this is because her father's beholden to me. We've worked out a deal, he and I, but I can't negotiate as I'd wanted to because his loan's current. Were it not, I'd *own* them, but that's not the case. If Eta's successful, I'm obliged to reduce the terms of his loan, and that's a risk I refuse to take. No, ye will guarantee it. I've already gone to the well too many times on your behalf. And if MacGregor wins, ye'll have plenty left over."

"The *exact* price, then?" Townsend hissed.

"Four hundred merks."

Eyebrows raised over darting eyes, face red, fists clenched, then slamming onto the table, knocking dishes and mugs to the floor, other patrons peering quizzically in their direction. "Four bloody hundred? The *hell* you say!"

"It's the best I could do, and even that's somethin' of a reach. Remember, the man's current. Ye dinna leave me enough time to work a better deal, so this ain't my doin'. And this four hundred, it's payable now."

Four hundred would nearly purchase the Ayr farm, and Domni's accommodation of Morgunn wouldn't run anywhere near that figure. In fact, he quoted the price based only on what he thought Townsend might be able to produce—though he wondered now if the fool could settle his debt if he lost without hocking family treasures and announcing his bankruptcy to the world. Such an embarrassment could end his political career.

"Mordiac," he said, now panic-stricken, "this scheme *must* work. I'm overextended."

"Ye've been overextended yer entire life. Perhaps this will straighten yer ways."

"Are you preaching to me, then?"

"Nae, that is not my style. That's just a fact. I'm helpin' ye for the last time, I am."

This, it turned out, would be true.

"Tomorrow mornin'," he continued, "can ye have the money to hand? Or are ye extended beyond that, too?"

"Nae, I have it. But would you reckon the cost? Are you sure?"

"Tomorrow mornin', or the deal goes away. Eta needs time to be settin' things up."

With that, Domni stood up from the table and gave a very loud thank-you, spun on his heel and went out the door, leaving Townsend with the tab. He then went straight to his office and drafted the agreement for Morgunn, before going to bed a happy man. If Ruadri failed to show up with the money, the deal was off; if Eta failed, he had both parties over a barrel. Life was good. He even fantasized about his own chances with her as he was falling asleep.

AT THE SAME TIME Ruadri Townsend was being presented with his dinner bill, the Ayrs were taking their evening meal. Morgunn had decided this scheme was an opportunity to relieve their desperation, but it was a family affair and would have to be ratified by everyone.

After they finished eating and the table had been cleared, he asked them to sit down again.

"My visit with Domni was interestin'," he said. "There's

nae *bad* news, but what he proposed has caused me some concern, though it could lighten our load a lot. I'll leave it to ye both. It will mostly be for ye to decide, Eta, but of course yer mother can refuse as well."

They were facing one another, the women now intensely curious, but what he said next confused them.

"The golf matches take place this Sunday."

They just stared at him. Then Olandra said, "What was it ye were wantin' to tell us, Morgunn?"

"The matches."

"Huh? What would Domni have to do with the golf?"

"It's the championship. It seems he has a client, or friend—or maybe himself, for that matter—who's frettin' about his wager."

"So what in heaven's name has that to do with us?"

"Well," he said cautiously, "we might could use Eta to our advantage."

Both women were now staring at him, bewildered. Olandra leaned back in her chair.

"Look at yer daughter, Olandra, so bonny a creature the lads is too scared even to speak with her. If she was just a wee imperfect, maybe she would've been gone long ago. And it could happen anytime, if one of 'em was to find the nerve."

"And *if* Eta liked him," Eta chimed in, the first words she'd spoken.

Her father nodded. "Aye, of course."

"I wish one of 'em *would,*" said Olandra, fetching an insincere smile from her daughter. "But Morgunn," she added, "what is it ye're goin' on about?"

"Domni believes Eta might could help with his friend's problem and do us a great service."

"I'm not likin' this then, am I?" Olandra snapped.

"Aye, nor me, but I'm not likin' our situation either, and this is maybe a way out."

"Is Eta compromised, then? To do somethin' we wouldna approve of, eh?"

"Dunno, because it'll be for Eta to decide. Domni's notion is that she distract one of the players—enough to make him lose the match."

Now Eta's mind was working, and her parents sat watching.

"Who is to lose?" she finally asked.

"What I'm told, Adam Paternis *must* beat Caeril Patersone."

"Caeril Patersone?" Eta said, frowning. "He's a shepherd!"

"A shepherd?" her mother echoed.

"Aye," Morgunn confessed. "I dinna say this was to be *fun,* and I'll not tell ye what to do. I'm only explainin' the terms."

"Distractin' a *shepherd*! That certainly narrows the possibilities. They don't take hints, ye know." And Olandra chuckled nastily.

"Patersone's nae just some shepherd," Morgunn told her. "He's beaten most of the better players—includin' that big lad from Crail, John Brighte, just yesterday."

"He beat John Brighte?" Olandra said.

"Twice. Last autumn, too."

"I've not seen him in—must be two years or more," Eta said. "Skinny, he was," which brought a glance from her mother.

"The lad's a player first, then a shepherd." Her father went on, thinking he was making headway.

"Morgunn," Olandra said, "what's this to do with us?"

He then relayed his conversation with Domni, noting that he expected him to deliver a written agreement sometime tomorrow. "I'll nae commit unless it's in writin'," Morgunn added, "and then only if we all agree."

"Aye, but what must she *do*?"

"He says it's up to Eta, as it would be anyway. What parents are we, tellin' our daughter how to go about somethin' like this? Dunno where to start."

"Of course not," Olandra said, with a sly grin. "Ye're a man! Ye're the *victim*!" She turned to her daughter. "Ye can help us, Eta, but please be careful."

Eta sat looking at these two people whom she loved so dearly, hoping she could do something to ease their burden. After all, the farm would someday be hers. "I've been meanin' to fix the baskets," she said. "Might could do it tomorrow."

Morgunn was confused by this, but Olandra knew Eta would have to wet the baskets in Swilken Burn, by the links where the sheep were grazed. She put a hand atop Morgunn's, which were folded on the table, and was reassured that whatever might happen would take place out of doors in broad daylight. "It'll be all right," she told her husband. "Let's hope Domni lives up to his end and brings us a proper document."

THE NEXT MORNING, Townsend dismounted at Mordiac's office, walked inside and, in the presence of the three clerks, pulled a pouch from beneath his cloak and dropped it, clinking, on his desk.

Domni held up the rolled agreement. "I'll take this to Ayr now and put the plan in motion. All will be fine, my friend. Patersone canna win. But I must go at once."

His behavior suggested he'd sealed his own success, but Townsend seemed almost grateful for his alacrity and said nothing, just turned and left with his head down.

Domni gave the clerks a threatening stare and said sharply, "Ye know *nothin'* of that gentleman's visit."

The Kitchen Table

THE MUNDANE kitchen table has been the most important piece of home furniture for thousands of years. It is more than a platform for meals or kitchen work. It is the heart of the family's world, for discussions, both small and monumental, and in this case it was where documents were signed. The Ayrs' table was ready, a continuous single oaken board, six feet long and two feet wide on a pinned trestle, with benches on the sides and chairs at either end.

Morgunn had counseled Eta and Olandra not to ask too many questions and promised to let Domni conduct the conversation.

The visitor greeted Morgunn at the gate and then dismounted, tied his horse and followed him to the door.

"Is Eta here?" he asked.

"Olandra *and* Eta."

They all sat at the table, as expected. Smiling broadly, Domni laid a rolled parchment on the table.

"Aye, the agreement," said Morgunn.

"Indeed, to reflect yesterday's conversation."

"As we hope it does," Morgunn said. "I take it, then, ye've been able to secure yer guarantees?"

"Once ye're comfortable with these terms, we can get on with the project." Avoiding the question, Mordiac had now made whatever Eta was planning a *project*.

Eta twisted in her seat with a nervous but very becoming smile on her beautiful lips, and Domni couldn't see how she could fail.

They went through the document, and each tenet was exactly as Morgunn had explained to his family. Smiling still, Domni was clearly viewing them in a very positive light for possible future endeavors—though of course the Ayrs didn't know this, and this mysterious, unkempt character made them all uncomfortable. But when the time came, Morgunn made his signature below Domni's, seeing this as an extension of their existing document, duly mentioned here. Domni, however, seeing it as a lump of cold cash, rose abruptly and began to roll up the document. "This will be filed at the Justiciary today, along with the debt document, but you, Eta, must take care to complete the commission. The lad's young enough to be—well, impressionable. Are ye ready then?"

Still seated, her hands folded on the table as if in prayer, she shot her bright blue eyes directly at him for the first time, but without moving her head. "I was *born* ready."

In spite of her incredible beauty, this sent a chill up Domni's spine. Here was a woman to be reckoned with. He needn't worry about her capabilities in the least, though his own hopes might fall short.

Morgunn walked him back to the gate, where they shook hands before Domni trotted away. Then he hurried back inside. "Ye were *born* ready?" he said to Eta. "What a thing to say! Ye're yer mother's daughter, sure."

"I am," Eta told him. "But now I have baskets to fix." And with that she was off, walking toward the links.

There was a spot along a small creek through the links that the local women called the *bathing burn.* Sheltered by high dunes from the bite of the wind, the north bank had just enough slope to catch the full warmth of the sun. Well off the beaten path, it was a fine place to bathe or work at tasks, like making or repairing baskets, that required water, and this was clean and clear. On some days any number of women shared the latest gossip while going about their business, one or two always mindful of the peepholes cut in the gorse by shepherds hoping for a glimpse of a naked woman. The women were aware of this but didn't complain unless the peeping became epidemic. And at this time of year, the water was often too cold for bathing, so they would just work.

As usual, there were numerous flocks downstream. Caeril was on his shift because he would be busy with matches come the weekend. He still had to pull his weight, of course, but he always had his clubs, and it was easy to tell where he was for all the featheries rocketing back and forth, as his animals grazed patiently, used to the commotion. But he was about a mile in the other direction, and Eta couldn't see him.

She walked slowly home, where her mother greeted her by shrugging with her with her palms up and eyebrows raised.

"Nothin'. He wasnae there."

THE NEXT DAY, Wednesday, Eta took a different route through the woods and came out along the dunes a quarter mile from the bathing burn, but no flocks were visible on the links. Worried about running out of time, she resorted to another plan.

. . .

On Thursday the sun was even brighter, and the breeze had died down a bit. Again, Eta gathered up her baskets like a trooper and disappeared down the trail. Her heart stopped when she saw flying golf balls.

A hundred yards or so from the flock, she stood and watched him intensely as he focused on his shots, facing into an opposite wind, and hoped he might turn her way. His fluid and athletic swing was a pleasant thing to behold, and he was tall and obviously strong, not the spindly boy she remembered.

When he turned, she immediately resumed walking, glancing out the corner of her hood until she saw him looking, and then she pulled off her hood and fixed her eyes straight ahead, her shiny silky-black strands of hair fluttering in the breeze. She was indeed a thing of great beauty, and Caeril Patersone recognized her immediately, though he had no idea she even knew he was there.

In spite of the worldly experience of playing in front of people, Caeril was still a boy at heart and had only once or twice seen the flash of naked skin at the bathing burn. He moved to the top of a small hillock, where he could see the head of black hair turn down the path toward the bathing spot, and his heart jumped. Though he knew it was too cold to bathe and she'd only be working on the baskets she carried, for sure he would have a look anyway. His dog was trained to stay with the flock, so within a few minutes, not far away, he went crouching to the prime vantage point. She was sitting on the slope, warmed somewhat by the low sun, out of the wind, with a basket in her lap, her fingers nimbly weaving new strands where the old ones had broken. When they were wet, these strands were much easier to manipulate.

Eta was scanning the horizon without lifting her head, pretending to mend the baskets. Before long she detected movement against the bright sky under the gorse and lifted the basket she was holding to her face, as if to inspect it closely. But she was actually looking *through* it, directly at the shepherd. After a few minutes, she stood up and moved toward the burn.

Could it be, Caeril thought, all in one week: playing Adam Paternis and seeing Eta Ayr bathe?

His dream was rewarded as she slid along the turf toward the water, her cloak and smock rising over her beautiful knees and thighs. Though it was cool, she kicked off her wooden clogs and pulled her arms from the sleeves of her cloak, which was tied at the waist, then loosened the neck of her smock and slowly untied the small bows down the front. She pulled the garment off her shoulder and began wriggling one arm free and then the other, sitting down at water's edge with both shoulders and knees exposed. Normally she would have bathed only her extremities, so as to not get cold, but on this day the idea was to be not clean but dirty.

Gracefully, she lifted her arms as the smock fell and ran her fingers though her hair. Caeril felt his body turn to mush in some parts, to stone in others. There she sat, her breasts in the full sunlight, brushing her hair with arms raised, thrusting her elbows back, turning from side to side in a timeless, sensuous dance. Caeril was close enough to see every jostle, in a spectacular ritual he'd never before witnessed. As amazing of body as she was of face, Eta dipped a small cloth in the water, wiped her hands and face, and then dripped water onto each arm and the top of her chest, where it ran down across her breasts. In the cold, her small dark nipples were completely erect. After soaking the cloth again, she caressed her breasts, and Caeril was transfixed—the weight and texture of her flesh almost palpable in his hands. Then she pulled her cloak and smock high above her thighs and began washing her legs: a visual feast for man or boy.

Then things turned comical. Caeril, physically and emotionally immobilized, suddenly felt something press against him from behind and spun around. His dog had faithfully moved the sheep in his direction and was nudging him affectionately—which gave him such a start that he jumped to his feet and instinctively began shooing the flock. Then he realized he'd exposed both his presence and his identity. He turned back toward Eta, who had risen, still bare-chested, only twenty yards away, and only now was raising her hands to cover herself, holding each breast the way Caeril would have liked to have held them.

"Uh, sorry. I was—ah, just mindin' the sheep and couldna help but see." With that he turned and resumed waving his arms at the meddlesome flock, as the dog circled obediently.

Eta had no reason to respond, but she could tell from the bulge in his leggings that her plan was succeeding. She pulled her robe back over her shoulders, relieved by its warmth, gathered her baskets and thought, with the same wry grin on her face, that she did indeed feel both clean and dirty. This was a vicarious thrill, and Eta realized as she headed home that the young man's appearance was more pleasing than she had remembered. Still, she had no feelings for Caeril other than the business at hand. He was, after all, just a shepherd. Now it was a matter of waiting until the match for her coup de grâce.

THE IMAGE of Eta boiling in his mind, Caeril thought about her with each strike of the ball, his practice no less painful Friday and Saturday. Nothing was wrong with his golf swing. Something *might* be wrong with his brain.

Matches

THE MORNING MIST was thick on February 27, clinging silently to the cathedral, as inside the haunting chants of the Augustinians echoed through the vaults and beams. The dew-laden close extended outward from the stone walls, and above it the huge facade disappeared into the fog.

But on this day, most people chose to celebrate the mass elsewhere, forgoing the gold-embroidered robes and jewel-encrusted croziers of ecclesiastic officials in order to worship with the contenders for the championship.

Holy Trinity was located in the center of town on South Street. Only a tenth the size of the cathedral, it had been founded less than half a century earlier by Bishop Wardlaw, in the same year he consecrated the university. Here the townfolk twitched in their seats, looking over their shoulders at one another and at the narthex door through which they would file out into the all-enveloping mist, bound for an altogether different celebration.

Hard on the final syllable of the benediction, Cummings, MacGregor, Paternis and Patersone led the way outside and turned right, down the path, each of them deep in thought, focusing on every step. At the corner of Merkatgait Street, they were joined by four others, all holding golf clubs. Two were ragamuffins clad in brown woolen cloaks, and the third, the eldest, Alphonso MacPhee, was dressed like a vagrant, common attire for an experienced clubman. The fourth, exceptionally trim and athletic, was Micael Carrick.

Together they went west down Merkatgait Street and veered right at Greyfriars toward the Scores, a Norse word for cliffs; then they turned left past the bow butts, where archery practice was held. Here, on a small rise, they came to the edge of the links and, after a few hundred yards at full stride, crossed over the Swilken Burn on the ancient stone bridge that was already over three hundred years old.

These eight moved at a fast but somber pace, as if determined to escape something in their wake, each walking in solitude without even glancing at the others as they moved though the foggy mist, leaving curling vortexes behind. By the stone bridge they were joined by yet another, who carried a black-and-white staff with a bright red pennant, but whose mane of white hair was every bit as conspicuous.

Following some distance behind, much less urgently, was a wide range of people, those in front clearly wealthy and powerful, behind them an ever-increasing stream of humanity in countless small groups that were not somber in the least. Lively in conversation and even with some muffled laughter, they lit the banks of fog with festivity. In 1457, the eight-hole star-shaped championship routings enabled the galleries to follow each match in its entirety, and the semifinals were scheduled consecutively so everyone could see both, including the other competitors.

Far ahead of the crowd, Gille-Copain led the small group

to an open area marked by a staff similar to the one he carried. This was the starting point. The clubmen had stopped some yards back, aware of the ceremonies to take place before they sprang into action.

The five men circled the pennant and officially greeted one another, shaking hands and exchanging nervous smiles and kindly words. Each was familiar with the others, and in this moment they shared an exclusive camaraderie. Here were the masters of their craft, players already tried and tested who stood together on the verge of legend. Clearly, it was their purpose for this bit of privacy that spurred them to distance themselves from the crowd. In fact, they were as diverse a group as Scotland could offer outside the nobility, but, in spite of familiar physical, intellectual and even philosophical differences, they were alike under the common banner of *champion.*

This is a world of very few but never of only *one.* There is always a *former* champion and always a champion of the moment, contending with *future* champions lurking in the wings. The nature of golf is such that a champion does not die in defeat like a gladiator, commanding general or king, so that—even years after being deposed—he may rise yet again. Likewise, a prodigy may not hold any titles but, if blessed with sufficient promise, he too cannot be excluded.

This small group, now alone on the links, included all of these. There was no anger here, no animosity. There were indeed many memories of victory and defeat, ebullience and pathos, but among true champions such details cease to matter after a time. And in this gathering there was a particular closeness, because their competition had been intense for a number of years. All but one was completely secure in his accomplishments, and that one was *almost* there.

"So," said Colaim Cummings to Gille-Copain. "What misery have you found for us this day?"

Angus grinned at them. "Nothin' ye canna handle, lads."

"I hope it's nothing *I* can't handle," Colaim added, "but that will surely confound my friend Nectan here," and at this point they all laughed.

"I hope ye know," Gille-Copain said, tilting his head forward as if peeking over spectacles, "that I *want* ye to do well—to be masterful, to prove yer skill. Aye, the pits be many and treacherous, but a common hack can handle the easy task."

Cummings eyed the ground for a moment, a trick barristers have used for centuries when searching for the right words.

"You have such a nice way with words, Angus, telling us to go straight to hell. But it's stranger still that we should be looking forward to the trip!"

Again they laughed, but the sound was muffled by the heavy air and the damp fescue.

"Old Samsone give ye a run, I hear," Adam Paternis said to Colaim.

"Aye, about like you've been known to do."

These men truly liked each other. Though the game had known grudges in the past, this group appreciated that at the highest level it was best played under friendly conditions. And, to these men, it was an article of faith that they all face the same obstacles—not only those devised by Gille-Copain but also, and more important, the ones they raised for themselves—and that no one of them was the enemy, merely another actor in the same play. While emotions could run high, unlike most everything else in this era they never took the form of physical aggression. Golf was clearly different, a bloodless competition at once athletic and psychological that featured magical larger-than-life characters in a primeval setting. It was as if the migration of the galleries onto the links occurred through a portal into a world free of war and servitude, where taxes, labor, disease and injury held no one in thrall. Moreover, anyone could play golf, regardless of station, and the game's mystique had cast a spell over them all.

The second group approached, and the players' conviviality reverted to stoicism as they sought solitude in the hillocks, their clubmen dutifully accompanying them as the crowd swelled and the fog began to lift.

The United Golf Honours Society felt compelled to exert over the game the same control they enjoyed in society. Without them, there would be no basso profundo introductions of the players, no commands for them to "Play away!" and no outsider joining each match as scorekeeper and referee, as if the competitors didn't know who was winning or how to interpret the rules for themselves. But the United Golf Honours Society did provide one important service, in that its most influential members always promoted the significance of the matches to the government and the church. In this, and this alone, they earned their position.

The current head of the society, Sir Petair Sutherland, MP, would observe each match, along with Domongart of Dumfries, the referee, though—given the superb condition of the links—there weren't likely to be many rulings.

There was, however, an urgent need to control the enthusiastic crowds, especially since Adam Paternis was playing. This task fell to Thomas Ross, the third in command, with the assistance of the local constable and various marshals.

Petair Sutherland addressed the assembled crowd in a rich, regal voice. "Today we play two semifinal matches. In the first, the competitors are Mr. Nectan MacGregor of Berwick . . ."—

he paused as a slight undercurrent rippled through the gallery, with intermittent applause, and Nectan stared out at them from under his blond eyebrows—"and Mr. Colaim Cummings of Perth."

The applause that greeted this name was more enthusiastic.

Sutherland, of course, had not yet given up the stage. "The first match, then: Cummings and MacGregor. Now hear ye! Mr. Ross has asked that you not crowd the play. Do not get in the way, and stay back from the ball, no matter where it may land."

In the past, Adam's ball had flown well over the gallery, only to emerge seconds later, bouncing back out toward the fair way. Conversely, on other occasions, Nectan's ball had finished among the spectators yet was *never* found.

The dense fog had begun to move out, signaling the arrival of a building wind, and the increasingly blue sky suggested that if there were any showers at all they would be passing. Still, most everyone surveyed the horizon and tried to gauge the wind, because weather was an accepted part of life and most of them were out in it every day, rain or shine.

"Now, if you will, Mr. Cummings and Mr. MacGregor . . ."

Caeril and Adam edged into the gallery as Colaim and Nectan approached the tee, both taking note of the central fair green off in the general direction of their approaches on future holes. Sutherland stepped toward them.

"I have here my good-luck groat, you see," he said, showing it to the competitors. "Given to my father by Master Walter Danielston the very day Bishop Walter Trail died in his castle in this fair town on—as it happened—the day I was born in the year of our Lord 1401." He turned to Nectan. "As the most recent reigning champion, Mr. MacGregor, it is your call for the honor to play first. King Robert's face or the Dumbarton Cross?" With that he tossed the coin in the air.

"Cross," said Nectan.

When the groat struck the ground, the onlookers could tell the fair green was firm and fast, as it rolled in a wobbly circle before falling on its side.

"King it is. Mr. Cummings?"

With an impish grin, Colaim glanced at Nectan and then at the referee.

"I defer, Mr. Dumfries."

A murmur went through the crowd.

Nectan eyed Colaim, who made a sweeping gesture, stood aside and said, "It's your play, Mr. MacGregor."

Cummings may have been regarded as a great gentleman for deferring, but he was also a wily competitor and knew that Nectan, having thought one thing after the toss turned against him, would now be scrambling to adjust.

But this was something competitors of Nectan's caliber could manage. "Thank ye, Mr. Cummings," he said. He quickly teed his ball on a large tight pile of sand pinched from the hole and retreated to well behind the ball to align the shot. Holding the club loosely in his right hand, he looked down to where Gille-Copain was standing in the fair way, leaning his flag to the right.

Nectan moved the five or six steps up to the ball, affixing his grip as he did so. The crowd hushed. He placed the clubhead behind the ball as a gauge, and, after eyeing the leaning pennant out in the fair way, took his stance. His waggle consisted of moving his hands left and right with the clubhead almost motionless above the ball. He shifted his weight from foot to foot, then stared at a spot on the ground in front of his ball. His body seemed almost frozen, but after a long moment his head began its familiar slow turn to the right and the grand arc began, culminating in crushing contact that sent his ball off at a stunning rate, high and far. The crowd let out a gasp.

As the ball sailed perfectly on line and settled next to Gille-Copain, Nectan—also ever the gamesman—stepped back and said, "Now it's *yer* play, Mr. Cummings."

"A nice shot indeed," Colaim said, but in return Nectan offered only his now familiar expression, in which the corners of his mouth turned downward, somehow manifesting itself as his own personal smile, part friendly, part condescending.

Colaim played a beautiful draw that started well to the right of Gille-Copain but curved back neatly to the middle, though not nearly as long as Nectan's colossal blast.

Both players produced spectacular approaches to within six feet. After much study and amid respectful silence, MacGregor methodically rolled his directly into the hole. The crowd applauded, but when Colaim curled his in as well there came a boisterous roar, not so much for Cummings as for them both, and for the lightning-like start to their much-anticipated matchup.

On the second hole, back toward the starting point, the wind now came from the left and MacGregor's tee shot found the tall grass. Cummings's hook was perfect, but his approach missed the fair green on the windward side and each lost the shot he'd gained on the first, both barely missing their fours, to great groans.

They then turned through the dunes directly into the wind, MacGregor playing a stinging windcheater and Cummings's low hook just nipping the tall grasses on the right. He then electrified the crowd with a long approach that held its line perfectly but was knocked down twenty feet short by the wind. Nectan, true to form, bounced his shot near where Colaim's ball had come to rest, and the gallery erupted as it rolled to within inches of the hole. Cummings's putt just missed, and he conceded Nectan his three. MacGregor, one up.

Each took a pinch of sand from the bottom of the hole and moved two paces away, as was the custom, preparing to loft the ball up into the great trailing wind, back toward the central fair green. Given the great height and length of his arc, and with the lead, Nectan was clearly in command. His natural swing was such that he could launch shots at different angles, whereas Colaim generally played a draw that on occasion was a downright hook and never got very high in the air. His downwind effort, struck much lower than his opponent's, put him at a disadvantage, with considerable trouble short of the green, and his ball hit the back slope of the pit fronting the fair green and kicked violently beyond the hole, nearly as distant from it as MacGregor's tee shot, sitting just a few yards short of the surface. From such close range, Nectan was able to lob his ball just over the cape to within a few feet of the hole.

But Colaim's magical pitch landed on the steep back of the fair green and then took a circuitous route toward the hole. Any slower and it would have gone in but instead it hit the far edge, hopped into the air and came to rest on the very lip, partially blocking Nectan's line: a stymie. If his play had knocked his opponent's ball into the hole, Colaim would be scored a three; unless his own fell in as well, he would lose the hole and the match would be squared.

Nectan and his clubman, Alphonso, scrutinized the break. Typically, he decided to err on the safe side, since a near miss would secure a half and he'd still be one up. As with every shot, he went into his ritual, holding the rolling club in his right hand and staring at the hole. Then he dropped into his familiar hunch, his great blond head hanging low from his massive body and behind the ball. After what seemed an eternity, he drew the club back and tapped it purposefully, but the line turned more to the right than he'd expected and, still moving at a reasonable pace, kissed Cummings's feathery and then charged into the hole, leaving his opponent's ball teetering on the lip. He gazed heavenward as Colaim, standing well away from the hole, spun abruptly away. Nectan retrieved his ball and then flipped Colaim's to him. Cummings now had his back to the wall, two down.

They continued east with the wind, MacGregor with another prodigious thump, but an ornery tuft of grass caught the rolling ball. Colaim was very exacting with his play from the tee, in the exact center of the fair way though again much shorter than Nectan's, but he rolled his ball neatly onto the fair green, while MacGregor's approach was thwarted by the heavy fescue. His third scooted past the hole and he didn't make the comeback: five to Colaim's four. Now MacGregor was only one up.

Turning back into the wind, Cummings maintained his edge. His hook worked perfectly under the wind, while Nectan uncharacteristically allowed his ball to sail, the wind driving it far to the right and well short of Colaim's. Then his low hooded mid-iron approach bounded across the fair green into a pit on the left, where the gallery could see it settle into what appeared to be hoofprints. He would have a hard time extricating himself from the sand, much less getting up and down.

Cummings had played perfectly just below the hole when Nectan entered the sand, his eyebrows knitted together. But it was not to be. His great strength carried the ball onto the short grass to no avail as Colaim rolled his solidly in for three to even the match and set the gallery abuzz.

In the left-to-right wind at the seventh, Cummings's hook held its line and put him in perfect position. MacGregor allowed for the wind, aiming slightly left, but there was a sudden lull and he watched his ball settle into the whins left of the fair way. Neither stance nor lie was onerous, though the tall seed heads of the fescue slowed and turned Nectan's club just enough for his approach to fall short and right. Colaim played a bumble, rolling the ball up the front slope to within ten paces of the hole.

MacGregor had to land his chip on the very front of the fair green, and his gentle swing just clipped the turf. The ball struck the slope, hopped almost straight up and then jumped slightly forward, with just enough spin to stop it a foot from the hole. A respectful murmur ran through the gallery at the delicacy of this shot.

Colaim's roll was severely downhill and had a large left-to-right break, with very little forgiveness. Then, just as he struck the ball, that same unpredictable wind nudged it on from behind. Colaim could only watch as it passed the hole and nearly stopped, then went beyond, ending up nearly as far from the hole as where Colaim stood, transfixed, a painful grin on his face. Nectan maintained a deadpan expression, knowing he'd regained the advantage. Cummings made every effort to convert the disaster, but his recovery curled around the hole. Nectan sent his home and was now one hole up with one to play: dormie.

Now the wind gusted in the reverse direction, right to left, and called for a fade, not Colaim's favorite shot. In addition, the fair way sloped down to a very large pit on the left side, so he literally had to bounce the ball along the right perimeter of the fair way in order to keep it out of the sand. MacGregor, on the other hand, knew that his natural fade allowed him to hit it hard down the middle, which he did, well clear of the sand. Colaim played exactly as he knew he must, and still his ball bounded and rolled dangerously toward the pit. It finally stopped a foot from the ragged edge where he'd have to stand to play his approach.

Both players had perfect lines to the fair green, Cummings some fifteen paces farther away, and despite his precarious stance he lived up to his billing, whistling his approach just eight steps past the hole, sending Gille-Copain dashing. Nor was Nectan to be denied. He too brought the ball in close; his stopped within ten paces. The two would find conclusion in the part of the game whose goal is decidedly too small: the hole itself. Nectan was away, and his play just slid past on the high side to a host of groans, stopping within a tap, which brought Colaim to his judgment. Having eyed the line with his clubman, he knew it was makable.

Then a very faint expression on Colaim's face caused a sudden sense of foreboding in Nectan, and after so many years and matches, dividing championships and regional matches, his thoughts moved to compassion for the person he now saw as his friend. Nectan *knew* Colaim was going to miss but for some reason the championship at that moment wasn't nearly as important as his appreciation for this man who'd never failed to make him play his very best.

The expression was real. Colaim did indeed feel pain in his legs—he'd mentioned this to Mary—and for a fleeting moment his focus was broken.

The ball struck the hole but with too much force, lipping the edge and finishing a foot away. The match was over. The crowd voiced their sincere appreciation. But something significant had passed in the space of that last stroke. Despite Colaim's smile, the sting of defeat was obvious as others consoled him, and his expression quickly turned bland. The innermost thoughts of both competitors would remain private.

Throughout the match, Ruadri Townsend and Mordiac Domni made sure to stay conspicuously apart. And while Eta was present as well, she tried to remain as obscure as possible as she scouted the positions at which she might reveal herself to Caeril.

The Sting

IN THE SECOND SEMIFINAL we have Mr. Caeril Patersone of Boarhills."

Caeril, whose head was slightly bowed, merely lifted his eyes. A small band of enthusiastic locals made a brief ruckus, but most—never having seen him play—applauded politely.

"And from Carnoustie, Adam Paternis."

The great roar that rose up left little doubt who the favorite was, and Adam stepped forward to acknowledge the cheers.

Colaim and Nectan had retreated into the crowd with their families and friends by the time Sutherland produced the lucky groat and stood between Caeril and Adam.

"Mr. Paternis," he said, "the committee has deemed that by virtue of your former victories you shall make the call. Please, sir, our departed Royal Majesty's face or the cross?"

"Cross."

Sutherland flipped the coin, watched it fall and said, "Face it is. Mr. Patersone, do you wish to play first or second?"

Being somewhat embarrassed, Caeril wasn't about to play Cummings's game.

"Aye," he said, "I'll play."

"The referee is Mr. Dumfries," Sutherland announced, and looked at the gallery. "Remember to stay clear of the ball in play." He turned back to the competitors. "Gentlemen, play away!"

Caeril was nervous but approached the ball with his usual ritual, and after barely a moment's delay he sent the ball off on such a good line that Gille-Copain actually had to step aside as it rolled by. There was polite applause, and a few encouraging shouts from Caeril's small group of supporters.

Adam pinched up his tee and placed his ball, and for the first time today the crack of the Queen's Cannon was heard. Gille-Copain just leaned back and watched the ball soar directly over his head, to a tremendous cheer from the crowd.

If Adam hit it like that on every tee, Caeril knew, he would be at a huge disadvantage. Still, his second shot whistled toward Gille-Copain, now at the fair green, and ended up behind the hole with a straight twenty-five-footer for the three.

Adam, hitting only a niblick, saw his ball stop perhaps twenty feet below the hole and clearly wasn't happy, jerking his head and slapping the shaft of the club and muttering something unintelligible, which was just as well, since the gallery included a number of monks and other ecclesiasts.

Caeril's attempt was bold and carried four feet past the hole; fortunately he was in Adam's line. Stymies being a part of the game, Adam had no choice but to miss to one side and leave himself a tap-in. Caeril agonized over his putt, but made it.

Teeing his ball on the next hole, he was confident he could stay with the great Paternis. Then, as he moved into position behind the ball to line up on Gille-Copain, his gaze was drawn instead to a pair of startling blue eyes. He quickly looked away. *Eta!* Recognition hit him like a sledgehammer, but the awkward hitch in his gait looked to the others as if he'd averted stepping in something unpleasant. He turned his back on her, his face flushed and his heart pounding worse than it had on the first tee. *She's here!* Visions of her beautiful milky skin filled his head, and he felt dizzy.

"Caeril?"

He jumped as though someone had shaken him out of a deep sleep and saw Adam looking at him strangely.

"Huh? Oh, sorry," he said, and moved back to the tee. He managed an acceptable drive, as did Adam, but as they moved down the fair way, Caeril could see that Eta was almost running to keep herself within eyesight. This in itself was not unusual because many people ran to vantage points when Paternis was playing, but in his mind Caeril was undressing her, mesmerized by the bounce of her beautiful breasts and the flow of her hair.

Watching his peculiar behavior, Adam quickly sensed that something was going on with this girl, partly because he too appreciated the sight of her. But being older, more in control and focused, he also hoped Caeril's distraction was to his own advantage. They were playing the like from the fair way, the boy again away, and when Adam saw him glance at her before he played, he *knew* something was going on. It was more than Caeril looking at a pretty girl.

Caeril needed to jump on his shot to keep up, but with his mind disconnected—as Townsend and Mordiac had hoped it would be—from regular swing patterns, it flew left into the whins. Adam, again much closer to the fair green, dropped it close. But from the deep fescue Caeril played a highly lofted, softly landing pitch onto the surface. Though they were still playing the like, Adam sensed he now had two weapons—the Cannon *and* the girl—and drilled his putt into the hole. His three on the hardest hole of the loop gave rise to a tumultuous roar from the gallery.

Adam teed his ball. Again, that twisting, slashing, athletic move brought forth another loud report off the club face as the ball roared off into the blue sky, over the break in the dune even into the wind. One hole up in the match, he was determined to increase his lead, starting now.

Caeril had allowed himself enough eye contact with Eta to form the notion that she had come simply to see him play, as her small, almost embarrassed smile suggested. The best he could offer in response was an uncontrollable expression somewhere between surprise and frown, clumsy at best and more likely spastic.

Now, though playing quickly as he normally did, he sent his ball on a wildly curving arc, far into the rough, causing Gille-Copain to turn around in order to follow it and then look back at the tee, as if to confirm that Caeril actually saw where he was standing. Micael began running toward the ball, while Caeril, bent at the waist, put his hands on his knees and dropped his head. He couldn't see Eta's sly grin but could tell that Adam had walked past him down the fair way. Finally he roused himself and took off in a totally different direction from where Micael stood waiting.

Caeril not only couldn't reach the fair green, he could barely move the ball. In a moment he was playing the odd, a long way from the green and still away. His third shot fell short.

Micael placed his hand on his shoulder as they walked toward the green, where he now could see Paternis's ball sitting about ten feet from the hole.

"Caeril," he said, "are ye with us?"

When his friend failed to answer, he said "Caeril!" again, and gripped his shoulder tightly, but Caeril just wrenched his shoulder free.

"Damn it all," Micael snapped, "slow yer pace. Is the Cannon botherin' ye? What is it? Ye seem not yerself."

"I'm fine," Caeril muttered in embarrassment He and Micael had often talked of girls, each with terrific interest, but to allow that this creature had destroyed his concentration would be a shaming admission of failure.

"I'm fine," he repeated.

Adam was watching from the fair green, confident that this match would soon be over.

Eta was eyeing them too, hoping Caeril wouldn't point her out to his friend.

Caeril was angry with himself, but Eta's presence so distracted him that his pitch caught the edge of the green and kicked so sharply to the right that he was still farther from the hole than Adam. Again he placed his hands on his knees—a position Micael hadn't seen him take since boyhood, when he'd been too small and too weak to draw back the bow that Micael himself used to put arrow after arrow into the target.

Clearly, Caeril wasn't blaming anyone but himself for his mistakes. To Micael, this was familiar. To Adam, it was honorable, and made him like Caeril even more. For Eta, though, the impression it gave was completely different, even dangerous. As he stood up to survey his next shot, an attempt he knew would be futile, Eta was beginning to see an unexpected maturity. Under pressure, he was his own man: athletic, tall and actually quite attractive, with a brilliant smile that had taken her by surprise—that is, until he realized she was at the match. His emotion—his spirit, his fire—was starting to have the same effect on her that her own electric blue eyes and rich hair was having on him. Had all been known, she should have left at that very moment. Caeril was clearly reeling, and her evaporation most likely would have ended the match on the next hole.

As it happened, Caeril's lag putt was feeble. He looked up at Adam and said, "Pick it up. 'Tis nae likely ye'll need three from there."

Adam, never missing an opportunity, glanced at Dumfries.

"Mr. Patersone has conceded the hole," the official told him, "so let's proceed. Mr. Paternis is now up by two."

Caeril's legs were rubbery. He knew he had to win a hole in order to regain his stability. He wanted Eta to go away because this situation was intolerable, but he *didn't* want her to go away because he had to know what she was thinking.

Mordiac Domni was moving through the gallery, spotting Ruadri Townsend across the hole. They shared a distant wicked grin.

Micael stepped in front of Caeril, forcing him to an awkward halt. Eye to eye, he said softly, "Caeril? This is yer game. Look at me. Do what ye know!"

Caeril nodded, and for two holes he hung on, holing from six feet for a matching four and halving the next with a five.

At the sixth hole, Adam stood his feathery on the little pinch of sand and once more fired the Cannon perfectly. Caeril, mustering all he had to keep up, took the same line, but a sharp blast of wind knocked the ball through the short grass and into a menacing sandy pit to the left of where Gille-Copain stood. His head dropped.

Hearing his mutterings of self-reproach, in which there was no whining nor an attempt to cast blame elsewhere, Eta could feel her empathy growing and her desire exploding. For her, Caeril Patersone had become anything but just a shepherd. She considered leaving the match, assuming her work was done, but found she couldn't; her attraction to him was as real as her guilt for his plight.

As the competitors marched down the fair way stride for stride, basically alone, Adam sidled over to him, grinning, and said, "That lass could stop a runaway rock cart, eh?"

Caeril looked at him in complete surprise, even more confused than before. He had no idea what to say.

"Laddie," Adam whispered, still at full stride, "I've had 'em do it to me too. Just dunna let it get under yer skin, if ye know what I mean."

This from a man whom Caeril wanted, in effect, to *be,* was clearly worth considering.

"Ye have?" he managed to say.

"Well, I'm maybe a bit more aware than most about what a lass can do to yer golf, Caeril. But ye might as well be wearin' a placard on your back."

Caeril felt like a boy just reprimanded by a beloved teacher, and smarting still, he said, almost as a question, "I . . . can handle it."

"Aye, lad. Then show me."

Caeril came to a halt, pondering this, as Adam marched onward. Was it friendly advice, as it seemed, from a man who for many *defined* the game? Or could it be a consummate competitor craftily pressing his advantage? Meanwhile, Micael had located his ball in what at first glance appeared to be a terrible spot, in loose sand. But then Caeril saw it was sitting up almost as if on a sandy tee from the bottom of the pit. They both confirmed the distance to the hole and Micael left to take a position downrange. The sharp lip of the pit and the ball's unstable stance were threatening. At that point, an average player would have been staring defeat in the face, two down with every likelihood of losing this hole as well. However, practicing the swing in that stance, Caeril could see that with clean impact the ball could clear the lip and carry straight at Gille-Copain, and this gave him some comfort.

Eta was also running the gamut of emotion: guilt, concern for her family, infatuation, hope that Caeril might recover and all-out flushed desire. Now she was the one in an emotional snarl, and against her better judgment she knew she would remain for the conclusion of the match. No longer able to turn away, she perched herself high on the brow of the bunker behind where Caeril was deliberating.

At this point Caeril said, "Dunno if I can do this," to no one in particular, though Eta heard him clearly.

Then, in the silence, the faint sound of her voice wafted down. "Ye can," she whispered.

He froze, staring out of the bunker, unable to tell where she was.

Again Eta whispered, "Caeril. Ye *can*!"

He spun around, and when he saw her his jaw dropped.

"Eh?" he mumbled, and with reddening cheeks he walked out of the pit, his mind processing this information. He'd already decided Eta was beautiful but unapproachable, yet now she was making an overt gesture, urging him on. "I *can*," he said to himself.

And when he looked up and saw her gazing down at him with a new and intimate expression, it re-created who he was. While simple attraction can be debilitating, when combined with affection it is a completely different matter. This realization bolstered his confidence about the shot, and Adam's apparent encouragement also rang in his head. This was a defining moment. He and Eta were wandering through a maze of emotion, her deviousness turning into support and his ineptitude to grand capacity.

"I can!" he whispered to himself, as he stepped back into the soft sand.

Addressing the ball, he could see only one result, even in that precarious place. The club rose to the top of his swing and down through the ball like some flawless machine working at something less than total speed and in complete control. The ball just cleared the lip and rose toward the flag, as purely on line as if Caeril was drawing its path in the air. He bolted up out of the sandy waste just in time to see the ball take a true bounce onto the fair green and roll directly toward the hole. For all he could tell from where he was, it stopped on the very edge, not six inches short.

Adam looked at the shot, then at the running Caeril and then at the ground, gently shaking his head. *Said the wrong thing there,* he thought, giving a wry grin.

Still running, Caeril brandished the club high in his right hand, then suddenly stopped to look back at Eta. She was beaming, her palms on her cheeks and her smile radiant as she slid out of sight over the hillock. He just shook his head—as did Micael, staring first at Caeril and then at the vacant space where the woman had been only an instant before.

But, as one might expect, Adam bore down. His perfect lie allowed him to go for Gille-Copain's stick as well, and true to form, with slashing violence, he took it in low and hooking, the ball running about fifteen feet beyond the hole. It was a downhill putt but makable, and a must for the half, since Caeril couldn't miss.

For the first time, Caeril was on the attack. Studying the line, Adam saw it would break faintly left and then right, and the slope made it touchy. One of the legendary rollers of this age, he had a knock-kneed stance and hunched over the ball with his head very low, almost as if seeking a fetal position. With a takeaway as deliberate as his stroke was delicate, he started the ball on its way and when it turned back on line the crowd began to stir. A low noise grew as the ball approached the hole.

When the ball hit the hole the crowd turned a mighty roar into an agonizing groan as the ball followed the lip, and stopped to the back right, less than a ball's width away.

Adam's face turned heavenward, brow furrowed, eyes closed, lips forming a small bow. His hands raised the club and pressed it against his right shoulder, a charismatic image that radiated his anguish to the crowd, his agony as visible as the ball standing defiantly on the edge of the hole.

All Caeril had to do was tap his ball in to go one down with two to play.

"On any other day I'd give it to ye, lad," Adam told him.

"Aye," he answered. "I understand. Thank you." And into the hole it went.

On the next hole, the Queen's Cannon was second, not only in sequence but also in distance. Caeril's colossal blast caught the short-grass downslope, which propelled his ball a good twenty-five paces beyond where Adam's came to rest, for once in the rough in a less than perfect lie. Adam had to go after the ball firmly if he was to get it out of this thick stand of grass.

Caeril waited. With a spectacular display of strength, Adam's ball, which had appeared to everyone to have been buried in the fescue, took off toward the hole. The fair green was just beyond a depression, and the shot flew to the very front, hopped straight up, and trickled painfully back down into the gully as the crowd groaned again. From there it would be a tough up-and-down, and because Adam Paternis wore his heart on his sleeve, his body language conveyed his every sentiment.

Now, with Eta always in view, Caeril felt he had an enormous advantage. His approach was only half as long as Adam's, from a perfect lie, and he again sent it to within a foot of the pennant, causing Gille-Copain to jerk the staff smartly from the hole.

Adam now had to bumble his ball out of the grassy hollow to keep from going even. His pitch, like his entire life, was bold, but his comeback putt neither fell nor blocked Caeril's line, who easily made another three. It was a new match and Caeril a new man.

Domni and Townsend were perspiring—as Eta should have been had she not been thrilled instead. The gravity of her circumstances hadn't yet set in. She was as blind as Caeril.

The home hole featured other horrendous pits, one to the left of the landing area and another on the right front of the fair green. In order to get a truly good angle at the hole, it was necessary to play close to the pit in the fair way. Ultimately, it was not possible to drive the ball over the sand, even with Adam's Cannon or Caeril at his supreme best. The only man who might have cleared this pit would be John Brighte. For Caeril and Adam, the only choices were to lay up short and right of the bunker, leaving a much longer uphill approach, or to carve the ball as close as possible, playing with peril but gaining the best possible angle.

Caeril still had the honor, and on the tee he and Adam exchanged glances of excitement. Both lived for these moments, which sealed the brotherhood they'd celebrated earlier in the day when all four men had gathered on the links; nothing like this was possible alone, only with other players.

The sole personal thought each had at this moment was that he would win. And now it was time to go.

Caeril set up his ball, took one last subtle glance at Eta and made his pass, going for the primary position in the fair way. Suddenly, another gust of wind kicked his airborne feathery far to the left, even beyond the gaping pit. It wasn't a bad shot, just a horrible turn of events. Seeing this, Adam immediately changed tactics, handing the Queen's Cannon back to his clubman. He no longer had to tangle with Gille-Copain's ominous hazard and instead took the ball in short of the bunker, assuming that Caeril's ball was unplayable or even lost in the gorse to the left. He couldn't have walked out and placed his shot more accurately by hand. The competition was now thick, as the gallery was keenly aware; everyone kept strangely quiet, as though viewing a chess match. Even the wind had died to a mere eerie whisper.

Caeril's ball had come down near a group of people, Mordiac Domni being one of them, whereas Adam would find that he had a great lie but a spoon to the raised fair green, being too far for his mid-iron. Neither player was in the provost mayor's office, as they liked to say, but Caeril was mortified. If he was within the spiny gorse, both he and Micael knew they would be as dead as the sheep who stumbled blindly into the plant just before dark.

The crowd flocked to Adam's ball, since he would play first, but Eta had followed the arc of Caeril's shot and came face-to-face with Mordiac, who glowered at her. A competitor herself, she was annoyed by his expression and now, realizing that her family was on the verge of missing a great opportunity, hissed, "What do ye want me to do—disrobe?"

Domni gave no reply, only an abrupt peevish snap of his head and a dismissive snort.

Eta fought to maintain her equilibrium, keeping her outward appearance as normal as possible, but her dislike for this man would only grow more intense in the coming hours.

Adam's stance and lie were good, but he had to get his shot up quickly to clear the first sandy pit and then carry it over the second at the fair green. There wasn't much depth in which to stop the ball with the grass hollow beyond. This was a major concern for Adam but not so much for Caeril, if indeed he could advance his ball at all. With the match hanging in the balance, they both decided to walk forward and survey the situation, crossing the fair green at the same time to inspect the hollow, though they'd seen it from numerous angles already throughout the match. Even within twenty feet of each other, they did not speak. Now it was all business. By then, Caeril had discovered that he had a much more serious problem.

Gorse—a very stout shrub with stiff, sturdy, needle-sharp thorns—is not friendly, and it has indeed been the end of many unfortunate sheep. Their wool becomes ensnared in the branches and thorns, and they literally cannot move. Even a healthy animal that's lucky enough to be found by the shepherd still might not survive the ordeal. In golf, gorse is the ultimate hazard. Even when a ball can be seen in the growth, it is not only inadvisable but also nearly impossible to get it out, and is deemed lost.

Fortunately, this was not the case for Caeril, whose ball was lying beside a plant, not in it. But as he tested his stance, he realized he couldn't make a full swing without running his hands into the thorns on the follow-through. This is why he'd decided to scout the area in between, to determine if he should chip out and have a clear shot in on his third but also to assess Adam's situation. Though he assumed his opponent's lie and stance presented no problems, Caeril knew

Adam would have a hard time stopping the ball on the surface, as Adam was already acutely aware, and likewise he was anxious to know what Caeril might do.

This, however, was a moot point. Adam really had only one shot and he had to play first, so he returned to his ball and prepared to hit. Caeril walked back toward the gorse, pondering his fate. Though any decision would be rash until he saw Adam play his shot, he kept making mock swings to see when his hands would strike the thorns. Not until after, he decided, the clubface struck the ball.

Adam could have played safely short and left and then chipped close for a four, but of course he decided to go directly for the hole, anticipating that Caeril, despite his difficulties, would do the same. He lofted an arching shot into the stillness on a perfect line with the pennant, the building cheers illuminating his excitement. If Gille-Copain had calculated that an approach from the lay-up position couldn't stop on the putting surface, he hadn't reckoned with Adam Paternis, and his shot rolled ever so slowly toward the very back edge, where it could've run down into the hollow, but instead, curled left, toward the hole, and came to rest just five paces from it.

Hearing the great roar, Caeril knew Adam wasn't thinking of a tie or extra holes, and he quickly forced the gorse thorns from his mind.

Two people near the gorse made their own deliberations. Mordiac Domni wanted the girl to get in Caeril's way, or whatever she'd done before, though he had no clue of the emotions that rocketed through the young people's minds. But Eta, who wanted above all to encourage Caeril, also knew that this would draw Domni's wrath. The outcome of the match was now entirely up to him. Back in the match, Caeril would have to live or die by his own wits and courage.

Since his angle was better, Caeril understood that the hollow behind the fair green was not nearly the threat for him as it had been to Adam.

He turned to Micael. "If I pull it off," he said, "we might not have to play anymore, if I get it in close."

"And what happens after contact then?" Micael asked blandly.

"I can roll it one-handed if need be."

His clubman looked him in the eye. "And with *no* hands?"

In truth, this scared Caeril, but he said calmly, "It's ours to do."

The hunter stared back, seeing not the wild expressions that had mystified him earlier but the man he knew.

"If it's yer decision, then. I'm with ye."

This part done, Caeril faced the ball with his mid-iron from a perfect distance, at which the clubhead could make solid contact, and took his address. But this swing was not to happen as fast as he liked, so he wisely stepped away. Then, leaving reservation behind, he approached the ball in the same number of steps and placed the head of the club behind the ball while setting his right foot and then focusing on the target, perfectly aligned. He'd put the gorse entirely out of his mind.

The club went to the top, on that line, and at the moment of truth—where he'd sworn not to flinch—the face met the feathery solidly, his wrists and hands pronating as the club released fully through the ball, which exposed the back of Caeril's right hand just before it tore into the inch-long razor-sharp thorns. But Caeril—along with the entire assembly—was transfixed by the shot's perfect trajectory.

When a ball is in the air, the best vantage point is initially from where it was hit, but once it moves past its apex, the perfect observation point is directly behind where it is headed, and those in between are merely guessing. The best judge then was Gille-Copain, whose practice was to remove the flag if it looked close, and in this case he did so and stepped briskly away. When they saw him moving, both players and the crowd knew it was close.

Caeril glanced at his right arm and saw blood and open flesh but quickly looked back up the hole as the ball bounced on the fair green. He couldn't see the surface, because the shot was slightly uphill, but there was no mistaking the ear-splitting roar that erupted when Gille-Copain suddenly pointed his pennant to the ground.

Micael looked at him wide-eyed, bouncing up and down and shouting, "Did it go *in*? Is it *in*, then?"

Many people ringing the surface were holding out an arm and pointing downward with their index finger, the unmistakable signal—it was in.

Micael sprinted toward them at full speed, but Caeril stopped when he felt the warm blood dripping down his fingers. In the midst of this maelstrom, he pulled one thorn from the back of his hand and examined several long deep cuts, hoping it wasn't as bad as it looked. Staggered by both the pain of the injury and the joy of the shot, he wanted at once to leap into the air and drop to his knees.

By the time he reached the fair green and saw his ball in the hole, his hand was a gruesome sight. Eta wanted to cheer along with the rest, but in her family's interest she hung her head, which Mordiac Domni did not fail to notice. Yet under her hood was a fierce smile of surly triumph.

Adam fought through the pandemonium and seeing Caeril's hand, immediately called for aid. "Are ye all right, lad? It's a nasty set of cuts." He shook the uninjured left hand in robust congratulations. "Ye must've wanted a win badly to do *that* to yerself!"

"Thank ye, Adam," said Caeril sincerely. "It's a great honor to play with such a great champion. Somethin' I shall nae forget."

"Ye make a fine addition to our ranks, lad. I only hope ye can take on Fair Hair with that hand."

"I'll be there, sure." Caeril glanced down to inspect the damage. "Looks bad, though, eh?"

"And I'll be there as well," Adam said. "Yer game's plenty good enough." Then he pulled him close and with a big grin whispered, "When you're nae lookin' at the lassies."

Caeril, smiling broadly, could only shake his head.

They all realized Caeril shouldn't tarry on the links.

The gallery, still buzzing, began moving back toward the town. Both Caeril and Adam were patted constantly on the back. A doctor appeared with a bag of supplies, and within minutes the cuts were cleaned and bandaged. Whereupon Cummings and MacGregor—whom Caeril had never heard called "Fair Hair" before—came up to congratulate him.

"I hope ye heal fast," Nectan said. "I dunna want a lame opponent."

"Nae, I'll play, ye know," Caeril said, "even if it kills me."

"Evidently," said Nectan, with a little chuckle, pointing at the bandage.

Together they joined the crowds winding back to the great yard of the cathedral, where stands of food and drink had been set up. Everyone was still carrying on about the hole-out, and Caeril soon found himself embarrassed by all the adulation. Again he shook his head and turned to Cummings. "Did they even *see* that first stretch of holes?" He laughed. "Playin' like a cripple, I was!" In fact, he thought, he *was* a cripple, mentally. With that thought he scanned the assembly for Eta, but she was nowhere to be seen.

Discoveries

IN HIS DELIRIOUS SPRINT to the fair green after the hole-out, and then in his concern about his friend's injury, Micael had forgotten to fetch Caeril's clubs, as he realized once the crowd turned toward town.

"Clubs!" he blurted to Caeril, and raced back to the bunker. It wasn't far, but as he approached from behind a large growth of gorse, his sharp ears picked up a conversation. The tenor of the voices was intense, and instinctively he went stone-still, as though stalking an animal, blending into the flora within yards of the clubs.

Though he was anxious to return to the revelry, the sharpness of these voices compelled him to remain hidden, and though he couldn't tell who was talking, he could hear the barbed words well enough.

". . . a fool I was to trust your cockamamie scheme. What do you propose now? This lad will surely send MacGregor packing!"

Now Micael was definitely interested.

"He's hurt, though, isn't he? He'll nae be able to play. There's no worries."

"Hah! It's only days till he's ready. I can't count on *you* for any help."

"Aye, yer lordship," the other said, sarcastically. "How short your memory is!"

"Oh, and now you're reminding me how many times you saved my skin—what, twenty-five years ago?"

"Aye, I should, but I'm not. Do ye think I'm the only one familiar with your gamblin' problem?"

"Gambling problem? Don't make me laugh."

"Aye, then, that's right. It's not a gamblin' problem but a *logic* problem!"

"I'll not listen to this! You swore that lass could distract Patersone. She was there, all right, but it looked for all the world as though she was spurring him *on*!"

"She did as I asked but it dinna work, couldna work, not against a miracle shot!"

"Aye, like the ones he'll hit next Sunday against MacGregor. How do you propose to fix *this* mess? Somehow he must be silenced."

"Dunno," the other replied coolly, "but it's nae my misery, not anymore."

"I can teach you what misery is, and don't you forget it!"

"What?"

"I'll put the justiciar down on you in two shakes of a lamb's tail. There's too many questions in your operation. What about that guild complaint last year? The only one who stood to gain was yourself. There are some folks you sure wouldn't want to see in the witness box."

"What are ye goin' on about?"

"Sithig."

At the mention of this name, both men fell silent. Micael strained to see through the gorse.

"What do ye want me to do?" The other man finally said quietly through his teeth.

"I'll let you know, but I'm finished playing games."

There was a silence again and Micael sensed they were moving toward him, so he quickly stepped onto the path and picked up a stride as though he'd been walking from the lane. When he came face-to-face with the two men, they eyed him warily, both visibly angry. Micael glanced at them, nodded his head and then retrieved the clubs and broke into a run down the lane.

He went quickly over the bridge, up the Scores, through the Pends and into the cathedral close, where he joined Caeril's group of well-wishers. "We need to talk," he whispered.

At a glance, Caeril saw it was urgent, and led him away to sit down on the grass. Micael turned his back on the crowd and said, looking at him, "I just overheard the lender Domni talkin' with Ruadri Townsend."

"The parliamentarian?"

"Aye. They was talkin' somethin' furious about the match and some lass. It had to be Eta Ayr."

"And what about Eta?"

"That she was meant to be distractin' ye but it didn't work. I couldna be sure who was sayin' what, but one was scoldin' the other for the failure. The other was arguin' that it couldna be helped, not with the shot ye made. A miracle shot, he called it."

"I knew somethin' was goin' on, sure I did."

"But what then?" Micael asked. "Is there somethin' you're

not tellin' me now? It was soundin' ugly, like they was about to do somethin' to be sorry about later. What is it you know, Caeril?"

"I know nothin' of that. But somethin' did happen to me that was strange."

"And what's that?"

"Seein' Eta at the bathin' burn," he said.

"When's this?"

"Just a few days ago," Caeril told him.

"In *February*?"

"Aye, fixin' baskets."

"Oh."

"But she bathed."

"In this weather she did?"

Caeril studied the ground for a moment. "I should've known *somethin'* was odd about it. But she's so damn beautiful I just had to—well, watch through the slot."

"Watch? Surely ye dinna see, did ye? I mean well, ye know . . ."

Caeril's answer was an expression of wonder and embarrassment.

"Ye saw the whole woman, then?"

"Aye," he said, with a sheepish grin.

"Ach! Why couldna *I* have been there?"

"She *is* spectacular."

"But Caeril, how many women are bathin' at the burn in *February*?"

"Nae many," he mused, then looked up. "I should've known it wasn't natural, but there was nae thought of lookin' away."

"Aye," Micael whispered, "nor could I."

Caeril was struggling to fit the pieces together. "Do ye

think Domni or Townsend was usin' her to throw me off my game?"

Micael considered this. "Dunno. Maybe."

"Caught me lookin', she did."

"What?"

"My dog come up from behind and gave me away." He was too embarrassed to say that he had jumped up like a startled child.

"So then what did she do?"

Caeril recalled that she hadn't covered herself as quickly as one would've expected. " 'Twas a show, I think," he said slowly. "Sure, she knew I was there all along."

"Did ye speak? How close were ye?"

"Twenty paces, maybe—the upper slot. Apologized, I did. Told her I was sorry."

"And what happened then?"

"Just took my animals and moved away. She wasn't there later.

"Nae . . ." His words trailed off. "If she meant to knock me off my game, it worked, dinnit? But bonny—aye, bonny she is!" He mused again. "For a while, it was all I could think about."

"Ye dinna think about golf, for sure. Ye chopped it like a hack."

"But then somethin' happened," Caeril blurted. "At six she started talkin' to me. She'd never said a word to me *ever.* She was floatin' up there, on top of that big pit. And I wasn't doin' very well, and then she changed."

"Changed how? I wasn't seein' any of this."

"Aye, she was so subtle, ye couldna see her start whisperin' to me down in the pit, tellin' me I could do it."

"Aye, and ye did. What a great shot that was."

"But Micael, she hadn't said a word till then. All of a sudden she was just different."

"I dinna see Townsend nor Domni," Micael said, "other than after."

"Nor I, but they must've been there."

"It's Townsend," Micael said, "who's the most influential."

"But Domni is respectable, is he not?"

"Dunno. My uncle says he was up to somethin' last summer, but he's not tellin' what. Just warns us to stay clear of the man at all cost."

"It's Eta," Caeril said, "I need to talk to."

Just then another group came over to congratulate him, and in the midst of the conversation Micael caught his eye and, poking his thumb at his own chest, signaled that he should do the talking.

It was a clever move, because Caeril couldn't argue the point at this moment. Frustrated, he watched Micael disappear and then contended with the admirers surrounding him and the quiet burning in his right hand. Still, he couldn't believe Eta had been a part of some scheme.

Money, he thought. *Fixin' wagers.* Suddenly incensed, he wanted to speak with Eta. His guess was that Domni was working for Townsend, but in his innocence he wondered why a parliamentarian would allow himself to become embroiled in a fix with a common lender. Was Domni that strong? Meanwhile, his hand felt like it was on fire, his mind swelled with the pride of victory and his heart was just confused. For the first time in his life, a woman had come inside the barriers.

ETA HEADED quickly home, sat down with Morgunn and Olandra at the table and told them she'd failed. Though they consoled her, thanking her for trying, she wept for the first time in years. Angry, tired and embarrassed, she said not a word about the bathing burn—but that was nothing compared to her growing fear about what Domni might do—and under all this were feelings for Caeril that were radically different from anything she'd ever experienced before.

She had seen a part of Mordiac Domni that was more than mean; it was ugly. She sat there fretting while her mother worked at her spinning wheel and her father busied himself outside. There was no conversation until Olandra caught her daughter wiping back another tear and went to put her arms around her as Eta stood up.

"Frightened, are ye?" she whispered.

A tiny murmur told her it was so.

"Is it that beast Domni?"

"Nae, not only him."

"Tell me, child. What else, then?" Olandra said quietly, but the answer was not one she'd expected.

"It's Caeril, Mother."

Olandra pushed away to look at her, but Eta wouldn't raise her face. Though she knew what she had to say, guilt from the outcome of this scheme held her eyes low.

"The lad said somethin', did he?"

"Nae."

"He *touched* ye?" Olandra said, with growing indignance.

"Nae, nae, he dinna touch me. It's not like that."

"What then?" she whispered, already suspecting what the answer would be.

Eta's eyes, now pink and wet, met her mother's gaze.

"Nae, Mother, he *quickened* me"—and this was enough to convey that she'd failed in her mission, because she was the one who'd become distracted, by falling in love.

Olandra again gathered Eta close as her shoulders began to shake. "Well," she whispered, "it's best I know," and she cupped her daughter's head in her hands. They stood quietly for several minutes until they heard Morgunn conversing with someone outside. They looked at each other and moved quickly to the window.

"Who's this?" Olandra muttered.

"The clubman," Eta said. "Micael Carrick. He was carryin' clubs for Caeril. But what's *he* doin' here?"

Morgunn came to the door.

"Do ye know a man called Micael, Eta? He would speak with ye. I'll send him on his way if ye like."

Eta was confused. Why would Caeril send his clubman? Was he too badly hurt to come himself, or did he not want to? Or could Micael be acting alone, on his own behalf?

"Eta?" Morgunn said quietly.

"Nae, I'll speak with him. But please watch."

"Are ye sure?"

"Aye, I'll hear him out." She moved to the door and looked out at Micael, who seemed agitated or worried, almost angry. She turned back to her parents. "Ye'll watch, won't ye?"

"I'm watchin', all right," Morgunn said.

Eta started for the gate, where Micael was standing by the hitching post. He looked at the ground as she approached, stopping a few paces short, and then he focused on her.

"What is it, then?" she said.

"Eta, I—nae, *we*—want to ask ye some questions. Can we talk?"

"That would depend on the questions. Is *we* meanin' ye and Caeril?"

"Aye, it is," he answered.

Quietly excited to hear this, she hoped the involuntary twitch of the corners of her mouth didn't give her away.

"I saw ye out at the match," he went on. "Caeril told me ye was cheerin' him on."

"I was, sure. Should I not have been?"

"Why not? Others were."

"He had a bad time for a bit—and then his arm—or was it the hand that was bleedin'?"

"The hand it was, but it'll mend. He should be ready for MacGregor. But Eta, Caeril said somethin' else was happenin' out there. He said ye seemed, ah . . ."

"Seemed what?"

"Well, maybe distant. At the first, I mean."

"I'd never spoken with him before, and he was busy, was he not?"

"But he said ye changed, when ye started speakin' to him."

"Changed?" She was amazed he could've noticed, with all he was going through.

"Ye said something to him at six."

"Six?"

"The sixth *hole*."

"Ah," she said, now staring at the ground herself, "how'd I change, other than I said somethin'?"

"He said ye went from lurkin' about in his line to cheerin' him on. Odd, it was."

"In his . . . line?"

"Right where he could see ye on every shot."

"But I wasna hardly alone, with the others about."

"Aye, but it was *ye* he was seein'."

"He's a very perceptive fellow, then."

"Ah, ye're difficult to ignore," he mumbled kindly.

"Oh. Would that be a compliment?"

"Um—aye, sure," Micael said, embarrassed.

Eta smiled. "Thank ye."

"But somethin' happened after the match," he continued. "I forgot Caeril's clubs in the moment, and when I went to fetch 'em I heard two men talkin'. Couldna help but hear. Fightin', they was."

"Who were they?" she asked.

"The lender Domni and that parliamentarian."

"Parliamentarian?" she said haltingly.

"Ruadri Townsend. I seen him with Domni. Aye, arguin' they was."

"That was *Townsend*?"

Micael eyed her as she fidgeted, starting to fit the pieces together. Townsend was the government friend that Domni had been talking about.

Micael knew that he had to go on. "Caeril told me about—well, uh, the burn."

Eta's beautiful jaw dropped. Her eyes wide, she stared at him. "He told ye that? Braggin' then, I suppose," she snapped.

"Nae, he wasna braggin'. He was *embarrassed*. He's confused, Eta, just as I am."

"Confused?"

"Bathin' at the burn in February?"

"I wanted to be clean."

"Well, we thought it strange—for the season, I mean."

"And that's why he's confused, that women like to be clean?"

"He said ye dinna—uh, cover yerself right away when ye noticed he was standin' there by the flock."

"He surprised me."

"Please, Eta. Townsend and Domni were talkin' about

somebody; *the lass,* they said, *was meant to distract Caeril from the match.* Sure, other lasses was there, but—"

Now Eta was staring at the ground, astonished by Micael and Caeril's powers of perception. When she looked back up, her eyes were brimming.

"Eta, tell me what this is about. I'm sorry, but we canna see what's happenin'. Do ye know? If somethin's goin' on, I need to hear it. What they was sayin' dinna sound good. I have to protect Caeril."

Eta brushed her finger under her eye. It struck Micael that she might be the most beautiful woman he would ever see in his lifetime.

"I dinna know who this Townsend was," Eta said. "Domni never told us the name. But now that we know—well, it's scary."

"Us? Who else?"

"Mother and Father."

"Your *family* knows?"

Eta just stared at him.

"Why's your family dealin' with the likes of Domni? I dinna—*my family* dinna trust him. He's nothin' like Master Dobarchon, may he rest in peace."

"Nor do I trust him," Eta said. "But Domni and my father, they made an agreement."

"An agreement?"

"Aye, a deal to reduce the debt on our farm."

Micael began sensing the complexity of this web.

"I have to know, Eta. Did ye agree to this?"

She paused, then looked him in the eye. "It was my idea."

Micael flushed with anger.

"It was for my family," she said haltingly. "But I'm sorry. And when Caeril was doin' poorly, I started feelin' . . ."

Micael gestured her to continue.

"Feelin' what?" he said.

Unable to tell him the truth, she said, "Feelin'—uh, *sorry* for him."

"Because he was doin' poorly?"

"Aye," she said quietly. "And I—ah, I felt bad."

"You did? Why?"

"It was my fault."

Micael appeared to be looking for something in the trees. "So it was yerself they was talkin' about?"

Again her eyes filled, and there came a tiny "Aye."

"What else do ye know?" Micael asked softly, still angry about what she'd done but sorry for her anguish. Then Eta surprised him.

"Would ye come inside?" she said.

"Inside?"

"Please. They're caught up in this, and our home's at risk. Ye need to tell them what you and Caeril know."

"They heard of the burn, then?"

"Nae! Please, dunna say a word about that!"

"Aye."

When Eta turned toward the house, Olandra could see she was upset, and she was surprised when Micael followed her up the path. At the door, Eta came in first and saw her parents standing there.

Olandra went to her. "Are you all right, child?"

"Nae, Mother."

Morgunn moved a little closer.

"Mother, Micael is here because he overheard a conversation we all need to know about."

Her father asked Micael to sit, courteously but sternly.

"It was after the match," he began, "and I came across the lender Domni arguin' with Ruadri Townsend."

"Townsend?" Morgunn interrupted.

"Aye." Micael replied.

"Are ye sure, lad?"

"Upon my oath."

Then Eta chimed in, her eyes now dry. "Domni, when he was here, was talkin' about somebody overextended on the match."

"Now we know; it's Townsend," Morgunn said. "It's *his* problem."

"Aye, a gamblin' problem," Micael said. "I heard those very words in their argument."

They were all trying to imagine how much money it would take to put a noble in debt over his head when Eta added, "And he asked me to distract Caeril."

"Eta!" Morgunn blurted.

"It's all right, Father. I want Micael to know this."

"Why?"

"Calm yourself, Morgunn," added Olandra.

"So he can explain it to Caeril," Eta said. "I was afraid of Domni already, and then Micael overheard 'em talkin' about me not doin' what was promised. There's no tellin' what Domni might do."

"From what I heard, Eta," Micael added, "I'd worry more about Townsend. I couldn't tell exactly who was sayin' what, but I think it was him made most of the threats."

"What now?" Morgunn said.

"I have to get to Caeril, soon. I fear Townsend wishes to harm him."

"You're his clubman," Morgunn said, as if to ask of his protective qualifications.

"I'm a hunter," he replied.

"What's yer family name, Micael?"

"Carrick, sir."

"Micael Carrick. Ah, ye won the Fife Meet last fall."

"Three years runnin', sir."

"Ye *can* protect him then, can't ye?"

"Aye," Micael said again, "and will."

"Why?"

"They grew up together, Father," Eta said, surprising both her parents; a slight grin creased Olandra's face.

"That is so," Micael added.

"What shall *we* do?" Morgunn asked him.

"Ye must be vigilant, but I must find Caeril now."

He rose from the table, and Morgunn stood up beside him and extended his hand. "Thank ye, lad. Ye'll always be welcome here."

Micael strode quickly out the door, but Eta went after him and called as he reached the gate, where he stopped and turned around. "Tell him," she said "That, uh . . ."

"That?"

"That I'm sorry."

"Sorry."

"Aye."

"Well," he said, "I believe ye are."

And with that he was gone as fast as a man on horseback. Eta returned to the house where the Ayrs sat stunned, almost paralyzed, but grateful for the sunlight.

MICAEL HAD NO TROUBLE finding Caeril, who was still at the cathedral, now being looked at by a doctor from Perth, in town to see the matches.

"I'm sorry, sir," Micael told him, "but we've things needin' immediate attention."

The doctor could see the urgency in his eyes, and advised Caeril to rinse the cuts daily—clean water, mind you, no animals upstream. Caeril said he understood and appreciated his help, and he and Micael disappeared toward the harbor.

Micael explained all he'd learned, concluding that he now had two concerns, Caeril's safety and that of the Ayrs.

"So Eta's bath was a performance," Caeril said, smiling.

" 'Twas, and one that nearly did you in, brother."

"Either way, she knew she would have to deal with me sooner or later."

"Caeril, that'll have to wait. There's dark things afoot. Ye must stay where I put ye tonight, and nae move."

"Where's that?"

"Camp."

War

THE CAMP WAS to the west, in the great wood that once covered much of Scotland, though now many trees had been timbered for buildings and ships. Micael made his living here, though so solitary was his nature that no one was aware of it. He'd brought food along for Caeril, and plenty of weapons were stashed about in the unlikely event that someone would stumble on the place. Small, thoroughly camouflaged and far off any beaten path, it was a perfectly safe haven.

Still, Caeril could think only of one thing, "I want to see her," he said, as they went on their way.

Micael looked at him. "I know ye do. But wait." He knew that a connection had been made on the links that day and guessed that Eta, having arrived with purely mercenary thoughts, had soon fallen prey to the same sickness afflicting Caeril. But at the moment such feelings were dangerous, so distracting that each would be a sitting duck for whomever wished them harm. Fortunately, Micael was a hunter, not a matchmaker, and this evening would be anything but amorous.

After a long trek through the dark primeval forest, they

reached his camp. Caeril had visited many times over the years, but never when Micael was absent. Once more, his friend told him this plan was essential, concluding with, "I'm a good clubman, lookin' out for my man. Just stay put."

Caeril studied his friend, having no idea of what he was about to do. Neither, in fact, did Micael, but he knew his bent this night might be deadly and involve moving targets, for which he had to prepare himself. When Micael left camp, he was first and foremost a hunter.

EARLIER IN THE DAY, another set of ears had overheard a different part of the conversation between Domni and Townsend.

As soon as Caeril's ball fell into the hole, Eta had spun around to leave—suddenly fearful of what this might mean for her parents' safety—and inadvertently came up behind Domni and a man she didn't know. Their talk was so animated and angry that they didn't notice her.

The strange man said that because Domni's scheme had been such a ridiculous failure he'd now have to swing into action himself. "I'll take care of that shepherd," he hissed.

They turned to find Eta standing very close by, and obviously she'd heard at least the last bit. Domni lunged for her, but she—far too quick for some gout-infested old man—was fast off toward home. Not, however, before she heard the other man growl, "Her too."

Eta, petrified, would never tell her parents about this. Instead, she planned on staying up all night to stand guard, giving no thought to what might happen if some malefactor actually appeared. She had no idea that Micael would soon arrive at her door, and now, long after the sun had set and so much else had happened, she was sitting in a dark room with those she would do anything to protect.

"Well," her mother said, "I'm goin' to bed, then."

Eta told her she would stay up awhile and her father said he wasn't sleepy either.

He sat in the glow of a single candle at the table, and she took a chair beside him. "Father?"

"Aye, child."

"Aren't ye goin' to bed?"

"Dunno."

"Don't," she said.

Morgunn knew then she was afraid, though not why or to what degree.

AT THAT VERY MOMENT, coming up the edges of New Pig Lane, were three faintly moonlit figures, fresh from a raid on Caeril's small solitary cabin several miles away. They had left it in flames and the fire wagon in action, thus distracting attention from their present activity, and the rustle of the branches in the slight breeze masked any evidence of their movement. From another direction, two other figures had already moved swiftly down the creek and through the fields to the back of the house.

The conflict now developing would come as a surprise to all in the house and outside, except for the two archers, positioned in the dark trees out back, where no one could enter or leave the house without being seen. The light changed as clouds drifted across the moon and a fresh breeze came up, but the two men with their trained eyes could still see the approaching band and began to draw their longbows stealthily in anticipation. The three figures on the lane were armed with knives, and one carried a rope. As they dashed toward the door, that same breeze masked the sound of hissing arrows and two deadly thuds. The cries of anguish, however, alerted everyone, and the battle was on. One man was pinned to the hitching post, another writhing on the ground, while the third, reeling in confusion, burst through the door, a grotesque vision in the light of the candle, dirty and seemingly crazed, with a disfigured face. Morgunn and Eta had already backed against the wall. The man moved forward. He was panting, grinning wildly, an almost toothless maniac, deftly passing a long knife back and forth from hand to hand. Morgunn pulled Eta behind him and lifted a bench in defense.

Then another man hurtled inside with a shout, also brandishing a knife. The first turned, surprised, but before he could react a grotesque agony erupted in his gut as a long knife ripped from just below his rope belt through his chest to his neck. The body crumpled to the floor, innards pouring from the cleaved gash, eyes staring confusedly up at his destructor until they slowly closed. Eta screamed, and Olandra came through the bedroom doorway and joined her.

Micael stood there, the Ayrs looking at him in horror. They realized he'd just saved their lives, though with a ferocity they'd rather not have witnessed.

"Now what do we do?" Morgunn mumbled, still in shock.

"Dunno, but I've a friend outside. We took down two others at the gate. We think there was only three, so they're finished. My friend'll take care of 'em."

The Ayrs were near panic, while Micael was like a prowling cat. He glanced out the door, and his friend gestured that one was dead and the other dying. "Let's move 'em away from the gate," Micael told him, hoping to prevent the Ayrs from seeing still more death about their freehold. Then he turned back inside.

"Ye must find a safe place—away from the house but not the barn. Just tell me where, so we might find ye later."

"There's a small hay shed at the edge of the north woods," Morgunn said.

"I know it," Micael answered, much to the farmer's surprise. "Go there, if ye think it safe, and wait at least till daylight. We'll stay close, but be careful. Someone will come in the mornin', but don't tell them I was here. Say it was self-defense, whatever. Have ye knife or bow?"

"Aye, both," Morgunn said.

"Can you use 'em?"

"Not so well as yerself."

"Nonetheless, keep 'em at hand and hope ye dunna need 'em."

The other archer told Micael that one marauder had gurgled Townsend's name with his last breath, which only confirmed what everyone knew. Then the two escorted the Ayrs to the hay shed, Micael sitting with them for several hours while the other stood guard. Once he was confident another assault wasn't forthcoming, Micael told Morgunn they'd circle the farm again to be sure the Ayrs were alone, and then he vaporized, leaving his compatriot posted in the woods behind.

Had Micael's path not led away from New Pig Lane, he would have come across Domni stumbling through the darkness. Hearing the screams of both men and women from a distance, he'd concluded that Townsend's men had fulfilled their dark mission and had remained hidden in the undergrowth until overtaken by curiosity. There were neither noises nor lights, so he decided it was safe to move toward the house through the woods, as stealthily as an overweight middle-aged man could. Seeing no lights still, he was certain the house was empty and its inhabitants probably dead, because the door stood wide open. What madness would Townsend provide next? This concerned him because at least two people, Eta and the clubman, had seen them together just hours earlier, though Eta surely was no longer an issue, and he felt only remorse at the destruction of such beauty.

He was scanning the house from the outside while these thoughts of dying women raced through his mind; then he grinned. If they were all dead, the freehold was now his, based on his lending agreements.

His meanderings took him near the dark barn, where the animals were quiet and their stench pervasive as usual. But he also thought he could smell *human* feces, which caused him to stop and peer at the dark barn more closely. Such places had always struck him as forbidding and unpleasant—even before Townsend had burned one to the ground, along with the livestock, in childhood—and if anyone was lurking there he had no desire to find out. In fact, he decided it was long past time to leave.

Making for the lane, he passed a cart where the odor of feces became even more pungent. There was just enough light to see that it had a load in its bed; but as he walked by, something limp brushed against his arm, and he turned to see a dark form protruding from under the side rail. On closer inspection he discovered fingers, attached to a hand, attached to an arm. As if he'd been struck a powerful blow, he flew backwards, banging into the fence behind him and staring, frozen, at the black heap in the cart. His eyes cut from the barn to the house and then back again to the cart, where he thought he could detect even more bodies. Unable to process these ghastly visions, he panicked. First he'd smelled human feces; then he felt a human appendage; now he thought he was looking at a pile of corpses. And in the silence he could distinctly hear a dripping sound, of either water or—as he guessed correctly—blood.

His body contorted, and he turned along the fence and broke into a run, falling several times before stumbling onto the lane, and within the hour he was safe in his own house, but tormented by grotesque visions and dozing fitfully in his chair by the fire.

THE NEXT MORNING, Mordiac Domni was awakened early by a loud banging. It took a few seconds to bring everything into focus, and even as he trundled toward the door, still fully dressed, he was piecing together the events of the night before: stumbling around in the woods, unseen shouts and screams, that hand and the pile of bodies in the cart, his godless panic. The bar latch slid back as he pulled the release cord.

Facing him was Townsend, whose condition didn't appear to be any better than Domni's, perhaps worse. The difference was that Townsend, who'd also sat up all night, had done so with the aid of liquid substances. Drunk, barely standing, he fell through the door and collapsed against the mantel, from which he fixed Domni with a deranged expression.

"My sortie failed to report back to me last night," he said, "as they were supposed to, once it was done. When I hear from the bastards, I'll give them a bloody piece of my mind for sure."

"They won't be needin' that," Domni said, now positive that his *sortie* was piled in the back of a cart.

Townsend wouldn't have understood this comment even if he'd been sober. But he stared at Domni as if he were unveiling some great mystery. "Aye, the match," he finally wailed, having misread the situation entirely. "MacGregor will *lose,* and I still must do something. I'll be *destroyed*!"

"Ye have an even chance." Domni shrugged. "Why not just leave it be and accept the consequences?"

As drunk with his own power as he was with single malt, Townsend staggered forward and roared, "I never accept! I *control!*" at the top of his lungs.

"Ye need to go home and rest," Domni snapped. "Ye canna think in your condition."

"I don't *have* to think!" he shouted, stumbling as he waved his arms madly, finally thumping his hands on Domni's table. "I *tell*! I tell people what I bloody want, scum such as yourself, and you either do it or else!"

Domni, now well beyond his breaking point, stepped quietly around the table and grabbed Townsend by the back of the collar. With his other hand he took his elbow, marched him across the room and smashed his face into the back of the door. Still holding his collar and now twisting his arm behind him, Domni pressed his own face up to Townsend's from behind his shoulder.

"Fool! Moron! The most you've ever been is *lucky,* and that's mostly because of *me!* Well, fool, from now on I don't know ye. Ye'll have to find yer way alone or use some other poor bastard to cover yer tracks."

"Ye can't speak to me like this. I'll have ye *jailed*!"

"For *what?* Ye're nothin' yerself and ye have nothin'."

"Sithig. I'll put Sithig in the box. The judges will strip ye right down. Then *ye'll* be the one with nothing."

"Wrong again, fool, Sithig's dead! I found out yesterday

after the match. Dead, ye hear me? Ye've nae proof of the first bloody thing, ye ruined, meaningless waste. 'Tis I who will burn ye—at the political stake—and don't doubt me." With that, Domni released his arm, unlatched the door and literally threw him out into the lane.

There was still no one about, and Townsend clumsily maneuvered his horse into a position where he might mount it. Then, from horseback, listing severely, he launched one more salvo.

" 'Tis I who'll do the burning!" he roared.

"Nae likely. I have records, fool, records of every one of yer sins. I'll ruin ye if ye even so much as mention my name. I know ye nae more. Are ye deaf?"

Townsend stared at him. Even in his altered state, he was signing Domni's death warrant in his own mind as he clumsily reined in his horse. "We'll see," was all he said, but with a vicious bone-chilling grin. And with that he cantered away, barely able to remain upright.

Domni stood looking after him, shaking there on his own stoop, wondering if Townsend would remember his threat or if he should have made it at all. Glancing up and down the street—empty, thank God—he prayed Townsend would not make it home.

Safety

DRUNKS CAN DO amazing things, whether they be eloquent speeches by the normally tongue-tied or feats of athleticism by clumsy oafs. Such was the case with Townsend. His horse, knowing the route, cantered straightaway for home, which was exceptional only in that its rider remained upright in the saddle. He was aware only of the cool air in his face, with no thought other than of sleep. His rant now delivered, he was expunged of his agonies for the moment, and exhaustion set in as his animal moved along the dirt road, leaving the centerline only to cut a corner, Townsend merely a passenger.

At this moment a ten-year-old boy—on a serious mission at daybreak and not expecting anyone on the street at so early an hour—was unwittingly on a collision course with the horse and its nearly comatose rider. Focused only on his duty, he rounded the corner to the constable's depot and found himself head-to-head with Townsend's fast-moving steed.

There were three minds present at this event: Townsend, the boy and the horse. The first wasn't really there, at least in the cognitive sense; the boy was consumed by his obligations; and the last was intent only on returning to its stall. This sudden conjunction provoked a typical reaction, and the athleticism of all parties averted a tragedy. The animal shied abruptly, moving hard to the left. The wide-eyed boy, to avoid being trampled, made an equally amazing leap to the opposite side. Townsend, who should've been cast to the ground, instinctively grasped the pommel of the saddle and leaned outward at a nearly horizontal angle. Amazingly, the horse didn't bolt or stop but merely continued on at the same gait. Hitting the ground, the boy spun in another athletic move to see what would happen next. The horse cantered along with the rider's body leaning hard to the right, almost parallel with the ground, and had there been a post or a building Townsend could easily have been decapitated. But he slowly righted, as the animal moved swiftly on, and never had a clue as to his narrow escape.

The boy gulped a lungful of air, marveling that the rider had remained on the horse or, given that miracle, hadn't at least looked back. The near mishap so preoccupied him that he nearly forgot why he was hurrying about at this early hour but leaped to his feet, abruptly swiped his arms against his pants, raising a few puffs of dust and, within seconds, at full stride, came to the constable's depot, surprised and disappointed to find the door closed. He tried the latch—locked—and stood back, staring at the door in the dim gray light, confused as to why it wasn't open, and then started banging on it.

After a minute of this, an upstairs shutter flew open across the way, and a gruff voice filled the quiet street. "What call have ye to make such racket before sunup, lad?"

"Aye, sir, I'm sorry. Where's the constable?"

"What business has a waif with the constable?"

"I've a message, sir. Do ye know where he might be?"

"Depends on the message, that."

"Well, it sounded important, and it's worth a groat to me."

"A groat? To deliver a message?"

"Aye," he said, and this was enough.

"Well, I am the constable. Just hold yer wits. I'm comin'."

The boy stared at the now empty window, and in less than a minute the door below swung open and out came a tall, heavily bearded, fully armed man who walked slowly across the street, unlocked and entered the depot, pushed back a shutter and poked at the still-live embers in the fireplace, the boy trailing him like a shadow.

The constable spun around and stared down at him, almost sneering.

"What's this message, lad? I have precious plenty to be doin' today, so if this is a game, you'll be sure to pay."

"Nae, sir, it's not. I must tell ye what they told me to."

"And who's this *they*?"

"Canna tell ye, sir."

"And why not?"

"Dunno their names, sir. Never seen 'em before, those two."

"Then who might *ye* be, lad? I seen ye about but canna say yer name."

"Thomas, sir. Thomas Drummond."

"Aye. Yer father's the wheelwright, then?"

"Aye, sir."

"All right," he said, "there's a step in the right direction. Now, tell me this message."

Thomas paused for a moment, then swallowed. "They wanted ye to call by the Pig Farm. Do ye know where it is?"

"Aye, I know it. The Ayr place."

"Past the house is a field, and a hay shed at its far end is where the Ayrs are. I'm supposed to say they need ye as soon as ye might could go."

"Is there somebody hurt?" the constable asked.

"Dunno, but they said to find the cart by the barn."

"And why might that be?"

"Dunno, sir. It's just what they said, sir."

"Can ye tell me what these fellows looked like?"

"Just—like hands, I guess."

"Did ye see any animals round?"

"Nae, sir. They was just—well, men."

"And when did they tell ye this?"

"Only a bit ago. I was goin' to fish."

"All right, lad. I know where to find ye if this is some shenanigan."

"If it's a trick, sir, I'd be surprised meself. They was a bit—well, nervous."

The constable studied him. Though the boy seemed fidgety, his answers rang true. "One more thing, lad." Maybe he would follow this lead and find the men who'd sent him. "Have they paid ye already?"

"Aye, sir."

The constable concluded they were either stupid or desperate, but then said, "That's honorable, son, that ye've done as they asked. Ye could've just gone on to fish."

"Aye, sir. Thank ye, then."

It was the first and last civil comment he made. But it was right.

The constable rose from his desk, shooed him out and closed the door, but before the boy passed out of sight he swung into the street on horseback and headed for New Pig Lane.

At the edge of town, he stopped at a small dwelling by a field and called out. In a few moments, the shutter swung open and a shirtless man appeared in the window. The constable, from his vantage on horseback, could see a naked figure moving inside and realized he'd interrupted an early morning session. He said, with a wry grin, "Sorry to bother ye so early, but we've a situation needs attention to at the end of New Pig Lane."

"The Ayr place?"

"Aye."

"I'll need just a moment. Do ye wait, or shall I catch up?"

"Best we go together. It sounds—well, interestin'."

Shortly, the deputy headed to the pen beside the house, bridled the lone horse and led it to the lane, going bareback in the rush. Off they went, at full gallop, and within minutes they arrived at the farm, stopping at the large tree short of the quiet little house. The constable glanced over at the barn but couldn't see the cart from the lane. "The Ayrs is supposed to be down the field in the hay shed," he said, noting the house door was open. The deputy swiped a finger across his throat, but the constable just shrugged. They followed the path along the edge of the wood, and a man stepped out. The constable recognized Morgunn and, as they approached, Olandra and Eta, all of them looking over their shoulders into the woods, obviously frightened.

"What ho, Ayr?" the constable called out and Morgunn gave a small wave. Once they were face-to-face, the constable could see how harried he was.

"Why are ye in the shed and nae the house?"

"Thought we'd be safer here."

"And apparently ye were," the constable said, "Do ye know young Thomas Drummond?"

"Aye, the wheelwright's son. Why?"

"Have ye spoken to him this mornin'?"

"Nae."

"Well, somebody told him ye were here and we should come. Do ye know who it was?"

Morgunn shook his head, not about to mention Micael's name. "There was a raid here last night."

"A raid?"

"Three men tried to break into the house. Stopped two at the door, but one got inside. Had to protect myself."

"If ye dinna want 'em in your house, ye had every right." Then he added, incredulously, "Ye handled all three?"

Morgunn, realizing how implausible this was, said two men had helped him in the darkness, but he couldn't tell who they were. The constable instructed the deputy to check the barn, and especially the cart, and in a few minutes the deputy came galloping back up the trail, wild-eyed.

"There's three men in the cart," he said, "and one of 'em's been gutted like a deer!"

Together, the men went to inspect the corpses, and since the constable didn't recognize any of them, he explained they would put the bodies on display at the depot in hopes that someone might identify them, not an easy task with the gutted man, whose wounds extended to his face.

"Ye were fortunate indeed to have protectors," he said.

"Aye, I know it," Morgunn replied.

"So who was it, then?" the constable asked outright.

"Dunno, wish I did," Morgunn lied.

The constable led him into the house, where blood and

entrails were spread across the floor, much as in a slaughterhouse, so they agreed it was best that the women stay outside for now. The constable told the deputy to deliver the bodies to the depot; then he was to clean the cart and bring it back as soon as possible because the Ayrs would be needing transportation.

With the constable's help, Morgunn set about clearing up the gory mess, but he had already decided not to mention Domni and Townsend's involvement in the raid. The constable of a larger town, or a burgh, would be an appointed official, a man of privilege, but in the tiny village of Boarhills he was little more than a watchman and a town manager. The constable's domain in this instance was common crime, domestic issues like property boundaries and, of course, enforcing the dictates of the local government and nobility, leaving figures like Domni and especially Townsend beyond his limited reach. He could contend with the operatives of the attack and the raiders but not with its creators. He said it was a good idea to leave town, but Morgunn told him he couldn't abandon the animals. To do so, he knew, might mean losing the farm altogether. He suggested instead that his wife and daughter find safe haven elsewhere, perhaps with Olandra's brother in the village of Cupar, to the west.

The constable explained that while the farm would be checked regularly, he couldn't post a man there round the clock; in essence, he said Morgunn was on his own. But in fact he wasn't, because eyes watched even as they spoke.

By now the sun was well up, and Caeril was pacing at the camp, anxious to get moving. He'd agreed to tend the flock today, but he couldn't leave without Micael's say-so. Then he heard him whistle the signal they'd used since boyhood—a good thing, because Micael was suddenly standing there. Caeril could tell he had news but he motioned, with his hand palm down, for him to sit down. Caeril took the only stool in the place, and Micael sat on a chest facing him. The first words out of his mouth were the ones he knew Caeril wanted to hear.

"Eta's family is safe," he said.

Caeril heaved a sigh of relief. "Was there any trouble?"

"Aye, three villains rushed the house. Barton and I took down two at the gate and got the third inside. One of 'em, before he gave it up, said Townsend's name to Barton."

"Dead, all three?"

Micael's response was wordless, a nonchalant nod.

"Anybody we knew?"

Micael shook his head. He told him about the hay shed and the wagon and said Barton was getting a message to the constable as soon as possible. "He should be there soon, and they was safe a bit ago. Townsend dinna likely send two teams, but there's no tellin' how desperate he is. His troops was gruesome characters, and I never seen any of them before. Oh," he added nonchalantly, "they burned your place to the ground too, but your ma's place is fine."

They discussed Caeril's duties and decided he must remain visible, so he set out for the pens. He'd spend his day in the links with the animals, and even though he looked constantly, he never once saw his protectors. It was midmorning when a cart rolled by on the lane leading to Cupar, carrying a man and two women. Caeril couldn't make out who they were, but one of the women kept glancing back at him until they passed out of sight.

Caeril's relief turned up at noon and he hurried to the Pig

Farm, desperate to speak with Eta. But when he got there, he saw only an old man putting hay out for the cattle.

"Are the Ayrs about?" he asked.

"Who's askin'?" the old man replied.

Caeril told him his name and explained that he urgently needed to talk to Eta.

"Morgunn'll be back tomorrow. Olandra and Eta'll be away for a bit, so Morgunn says."

"Where are they, then?"

"Dunno. Ye the golfer Patersone?"

"Aye."

"MacGregor," the old man said, "he's a tough one."

"That he is."

"How's yer hand, lad?"

"Should be ready," Caeril replied, and started back to the links to practice and test how his hand felt holding a club.

He was only halfway down the lane when he heard the whistle and Micael materialized.

"What're ye doin' out here?" Caeril said.

"Did ye think ye was alone, then?"

"Is it necessary," Caeril asked, "me bein' shadowed?"

"For now, sure, and maybe through the match. I need more information on Townsend. I know more about Domni than I'd like, and we can't take any chances. Eta's gone with her mother to her uncle, somewhere in the west. Ye have to let things rest with Eta, at least until after Sunday. And Caeril," he added, "it's best ye stay in camp or with my family, maybe move around a bit. Let's keep 'em guessin'."

Knowing Micael was right, Caeril resigned himself to living like a gypsy, but as the days passed, he changed. With his small abode reduced to ashes, his only clothes on his back, meals wherever he could find them and only a few items in his pouch, Caeril was angry. His wounds were a tender annoyance, and he was ashamed of his performance, now considering the victory an accidental gift of divine intervention, as suggested by Gille-Copain. Eta, in spite of her beauty and the obvious events at the match, was becoming an enigma, and he was embarrassed by the entire affair. He worried about what Domni and Townsend might try at the finals and wished it all away. In the end, perhaps more as an emotional defense, he dismissed Eta as something far less than she appeared. This time, he thought, he would be ready for anything.

Dobarchon's Ghost

As a political figure, Ruadri Townsend had many enemies, but chief among them was his own brain, which was capable of holding only a single thought at a time. He was now obsessed with Domni's claim to have recorded his every transgression, and certainly Domni had hidden the list somewhere in his office. This lowborn knave had known him his entire life, and no crime, no matter how trivial, would escape his accounting. In Townsend's stupor, this betrayal became monumental. Townsend had taken Domni into his confidence, which would now be his ruin—unless he took fate in his own hands.

Almost exactly twenty-four hours after the near collision by the constable's depot, a figure wearing a green cloak with a dark brown hood moved quickly through the streets of St. Andrews and down along the coast toward Boarhills, where one of the few freestanding buildings had served as William Dobarchon's office. The place had been regarded almost as a shrine and, upon Dobarchon's death, had been inherited by Mordiac Domni, who lived behind the building after a small yard.

In the early morning dimness, the green-cloaked figure continually checked in every direction before coming at last to his destination: the side of Domni's office that faced the links, where the shutters weren't barred and he could climb right through the window. In a matter of minutes, he came out the front door and disappeared into the links.

Domni, an early riser, had just completed his morning constitutional and was shuffling back to his quarters from his privy, suspecting that someone had run out of coal because the scent of burning wood was in the breeze—a musing that turned to horror as he realized the odor came from his office, where he now saw flames dancing within.

For the second day in a row, the constable was roused very early. He too smelled burning wood but knew immediately it wasn't from a fireplace. He pulled the line that ran from his home across the street to the fire bell at the depot; this alarm could be sounded from either location, as well as from the quarters of the appointed fireman, whose duties included keeping the water wagon full at all times and his four shires ready to go. Roughly seventeen hands tall, with broad hooves, these draft horses had long fetlocks that looked for all the world like fur boots. When not harnessed, two at a time in six-hour shifts, they grazed in the fields by the firehouse or fed at the trough. Switching teams four times a day, and filling the wagon almost as often, was a twenty-four-hour endeavor that required a youthful crew in relief, and since most disasters occurred at night, when everyone was asleep, the fireman generally dozed through the day, leaving the hitching and filling to the boys, so by this hour he was normally waning from his all-night vigil.

At the sound of the bell, volunteers from around the village set off immediately to the station or where the fire was burning, their priority generally to keep adjoining structures from going up in smoke as well. On this Tuesday morning there was no one on the streets, and the breeze was strong enough to disperse the smoke, but the constable cleverly looked upwind and, seeing flames flickering out the open window of Domni's office, raced to the firehouse beside the depot and helped to ready the wagon.

In the meantime, Domni's attempt to enter through the back door was blocked by shooting flames, so he ran in from the street side and began grabbing papers before they ignited. By the time he found the Townsend file, neatly tied, the inferno surrounded him on three sides, and the door—through which the wind now whistled—was his only escape. Still he continued to gather his papers, considering them no less valuable than money. The sod roof kept those timbers from burning, but the tie beams were fully engulfed and began to collapse, one of them falling directly in front of him as he ran for the door. His cloak caught fire, and by the time he leaped over the beam he was almost completely aflame. He stumbled against the frame as he ran through the door and the Townsend file burst open, wind carrying the papers in all directions, some floating back through the door, others over the roof, all of them afire. In a wild panic, he burst around the same corner where young Drummond had come just the morning before, and then he screamed horribly—for pounding down on him was more than three tons of wood, iron, water, two snorting shires and a wild-eyed fireman standing on the wagon box, snapping his whip and shouting among the clods of dirt and debris flung up by the horses' huge hooves.

This stupendous event was witnessed by the constable,

several volunteers and a few bystanders, one of them wearing a green cloak with a dark brown hood. The first thing that caught Mordiac Domni, now a running ball of flame, was the center tree to which the shires were harnessed, and he collapsed under it like a rag doll, sending the horses immediately out of control, one stumbling to the right and the other trampling his body. The rig hurtled forward, its heavy wheels cutting through the corpse thrown up in its wake in multiple sections. Then the right horse fell, and the left horse rolled on top of it and the wagon pitched violently, a heavy sheet of water shooting ahead to douse in midair what was left of Domni, delivering this bloody smoldering lump to the constable's feet. The unfortunate fireman had been launched headlong some thirty feet into a hitching post, which splintered along with his skull. All was a steaming mud-splattered silence, except for one slowly turning wagon wheel and a struggling shire that was quickly unshackled and led away.

With three deaths—two men and one horse—in a fiery mayhem, this event would live on in legend. But along with it went Domni's every shadowy deal, every lending immorality and every cruel manipulation, all vaporized in the ash of his place of business. Within the hour there was no trace of his corrupt occupancy. Perhaps Dobarchon's ghost had returned to guide the fire wagon on its way to scatter Mordiac Domni literally all over the lane.

At this point, the cloaked figure ambled down the well-worn coastal path back into St. Andrews, and at the corner of Buckler's Wynd and North Street he climbed the forestair of a beautiful stone cottage with crowstepped gables and a pantile roof, where he knocked and waited, glancing nervously up and down the street to see if anyone was watching. The housemaid opened the door, closed it after a short exchange, and in a moment Townsend appeared in a dressing gown to greet him. After his visitor said a sentence or two, he smiled, slipped something into his hand and started to close the door. But the man kept talking, and he listened with the door ajar, until it abruptly flew open and Townsend stepped out with a broad toothy smile and then a belly laugh, holding up his index finger to tell the man to wait. He disappeared briefly inside before returning within moments to hand him a thick envelope, whereupon his visitor looked slyly in both directions as the parliamentarian patted him on the back in farewell. Stepping back inside, Townsend raised a fist in triumph, and the cloaked figure soon vanished between two buildings on North Street.

By noon on Tuesday, Morgunn had returned to the farm. Less than fifteen minutes later, he saw Micael coming across the field carrying his longbow, a quiver over his shoulder, and waved from where he was cutting hay. He then stood motionless as Micael explained how Domni had died. Morgunn wasn't sure what effect this would have on his own debt, but eventually he discovered there was no confirmed note for either transaction at the Justiciary. The loan records dated back to the Dobarchon era, most of which were either paid or secured, but Domni was essentially self-funding and certainly had no desire to enter his complex mean-spirited agreements into the public record. Thus Morgunn Ayr was free and clear.

The next day he also heard from the flesher who had learned of Domni's fiery demise, asking why he'd not been bringing him animals to butcher. Stupified, Morgunn responded that Domni had said the flesher was too busy to handle more than one a month. And when the flesher relayed the lies that

Domni had told him, they smiled and decided it was time get to know each other better over an ale or two.

Later, Caeril sat in awe as Micael explained all this to him. "I told Morgunn his troubles was at least half over," he concluded, "but I'd warrant that fire had somethin' to do with Townsend."

They both knew that Ruadri Townsend was still extremely dangerous, perhaps even more than ever.

AT THE SAME TIME Micael was at the Ayr farm, Townsend was in his study looking out at the bustle on North Street, fretting about his predicament and assessing his life without Domni. Some of it was good, such as not having the lender holding him moral hostage. On the other hand, he no longer had someone to provide him with ready-made alibis. On balance, Townsend felt relieved. He was no longer bound to Domni's schemes, which had landed him in this mess in the first place. "I wish this match would just go away," he mused. "Then I could start anew, minding my bets."

He stood facing the window, and suddenly his body stiffened. "That's *it*!" He shouted, startling the housemaid. "The match! The *match itself* can go away!"

There had been talk in Parliament about the rising popularity of sport, particularly golf and football, and how the country's military prowess was a joke because of it. The Scottish people were becoming so obsessed with games, even at the highest levels of society, there was increasing concern that they'd grown complacent about independence instead of learning to defend themselves. They couldn't go to war with golf clubs, nor could they kick balls at the English. The gentry, this argument went, should be practicing archery, a talent at which the nation was woefully inept; if they were to be on a tactical par with England, they needed many proficient archers; they had the raw materials for it, and the talent to assemble the weapons, with joiners in each and every town. The answer was to ban games of sport.

A less self-abused man would have come to this conclusion in an instant, but Townsend was grappling with his own demise. Still, now that his thoughts had drifted unbidden to a new idea, he recalled that only last year a ban on both sports had come to a vote in the Parliament, having been sent there by James himself. On that occasion, of course, Ruadri had followed his wagering impulse and cast his vote against the ban, which failed to pass by only three votes. Those in favor, naturally, were eager to try again; and with success in Parliament they could then return the measure to the king for his approval.

Even so, Townsend was enough of a politician to see that King James might, in fact, be playing them all for fools. He could, by divine right, abandon the idea entirely and dismiss this positive new vote, thus catering to the many middle-class adherents of golf and boost his general popularity by defying the well-born lords of Parliament and, in effect, dashing Townsend's only hope of salvation.

But should the measure pass, Petair Sutherland could no longer strut around as the grand marshal of the United Golf Honours Society, so he was therefore the principal opponent of the ban. But Townsend now enjoyed the epiphany that with one additional vote and his own defecting vote, the ban would pass nonetheless, to the supreme annoyance of Sutherland, who was also his mortal enemy on nearly all other measures.

In his euphoria, Townsend searched his mind for that other deciding vote. Parliament was a matter of favors and allegiances and he felt sure he could sway one of at least three ministers, but since time was of the essence—the session would convene the following day—the closest option was also his best: Thomas Douglas, the much older stepbrother of Archibald Douglas of Bell-the-Cat fame and one of the Red Douglases of Angus, just across the Firth of Tay to the north.

Within the hour, Townsend was approaching Leuchars, en route to Newport for the short boat ride to Dundee and then west a few miles to Kingoodie, Thomas's home. Townsend had gone out on a limb, having given no notice of his visit, but his luck held. Not only was Thomas at home, preparing to go to Perth himself, he was also quite pleased to see Townsend, for his own political interest in broadening the fishing levies. Townsend's father had fiercely protected fishermen from this tax because it adversely affected the booming economy of eastern Fife, and his son had followed suit. This of course gave Ruadri something to sell, and it didn't take long for him to forsake his father on this issue in exchange for Douglas's vote on the sporting ban. So simply did the balance swing.

Determined to see his mission through, Townsend opted not to accompany Douglas to Perth the next day but to return to St. Andrews for the coup d'état. Though the vote count appeared conclusive, he wanted regal endorsement, and for that he would again fall back on foundations laid by his father—Bishop Kennedy. In halcyon times, the elder Townsend and the bishop had negotiated agreements that generated money for both church and royal coffers, not to mention a few in the nobleman's purse. And the bishop knew his friend's son not as a blithering, drunken miscreant but only as a well-known parliamentarian, following in the footsteps of his father, Kennedy's dear friend.

Indeed, at this moment, Kennedy did loom large. As the senior advisor of the Old Lords, he had been on close terms with James from the time the latter was six years old until he secured his crown.

Kennedy, as they say, could look the king in the eye. Without a single chink in his philosophical and moral armor, not an unkind bone in his body, he was an ecclesiastic and national hero. What he saw in his friend's son was a mystery, though he certainly recognized that his august position was, somewhat like his own, largely an accident of birth.

Upon arriving home, Townsend sat immediately at his desk and wrote to Kennedy, requesting a visit at his earliest convenience on a matter of national security. This he sealed with his stamp with bright red wax and had a courier deliver it. Before nightfall he received Kennedy's response; the bishop looked forward to meeting him in the castle the following morning. Amazingly, at bedtime, Townsend was the picture of a proud and sober nobleman, having for once vowed to be on his best behavior.

THURSDAY, March 3, 1457, was a day that two hundred years earlier would've sent Bishop Wishart and his Augustinians scurrying to bolster the unfinished buttresses of the great cathedral to prevent it from toppling in the wind; but on such a day, even all the armies that had combined to construct this edifice would have failed. Townsend had to call for his carriage or else present himself to Kennedy soaked to the skin and looking as if he'd walked in from Perth.

The small enclosed vehicle clopped up North Street, where he could see the cathedral spires rising in the rain above the homes and shops. At Castle Wynd, which some still called Fishergate, he turned left to the Scores. Once at the magnificent foretower that contained the castle drawbridge, the carriage passed through the great arch and on into the courtyard, which was busy in spite of the weather, owing to the presence of King James II in the castle. They circled to the right and finally stopped by the arches of the loggia of the chapel, though rain still tapped on the carriage roof. He dashed under the center arch into the chapel's narthex, then continued to the southeastern tower and the office where Kennedy daily spent hours asking for divine guidance in the many decisions of the realm. Pausing before a grand oak door on which the bishop's crest was carved, Townsend marveled at the detail: Mary holding Jesus at the peak, Andrew struggling on the saltire in the middle, with a small Kennedy seemingly bending under the weight at the bottom. Feeling the bold truth of this crest, he crossed himself before knocking.

Within a moment, a monk swung the door open and took his cloak. "The bishop awaits ye, sir," he said. "Please, this way."

Years had passed since Townsend had last visited the bishop's palace, and again he marveled at its opulence—especially the amount of money required to construct and maintain it.

Reaching a smaller oak door, the monk put one hand on the latch, tapped lightly with the other, turned and said, "Please enter, sir."

Greeted by this vision of arches spanning a gracious room, with tracery panels inserted into the vaults and small interior arcades richly embellished with decorative and realistic detail, Townsend for once felt the futility of his own existence. A large rectangular stained-glass window graced the east wall above a row of plain-glass windows; dwarfed by it all was the frail figure of James Kennedy, who was staring outside through panes so spotted with rain that nothing was truly visible.

Kennedy was almost completely bald, with a sharp hump high on his nose and eyes so clear and penetrating that

Townsend feared he could see inside his very soul. Gracious and affable, he greeted his visitor with a warm handshake and a smile, which Townsend managed to return. It was, in fact, impossible to believe that this same man, three mornings ago, had been clinging to his saddle in a drunken stupor.

"So, Ruadri, what is this matter of great national security, eh?"

"Well, your grace, it has struck me full force that we're pitifully vulnerable to attack from the south."

"You have news of such an attack, then?"

"Nae, your grace, but I see in our culture a dearth of readiness, a dreadful lowering of the guard. If attacked at this moment, we'd be woefully ill prepared."

Kennedy stared at him, knowing that this boy always had more than one agenda. While everyone knew even James's father had felt similar apprehensions, why would a nobleman not previously concerned with defense suddenly come forth with this idea? Peering into his visitor's eyes, he said, "And?"

"And what, your grace?"

"What *else,* Ruadri? And why now?"

"Well, it's Scotland's problem! Am I the only man who feels it?"

"I'm sorry, my friend. You will find significant support for this cause, of course. But in all honesty, I was wondering if there might perhaps be an ulterior motive. Is there, Ruadri?"

Townsend, though somewhat taken aback, countered gamely. "Your grace, the gentry is obsessed with the games. They plan their lives around them, and many bet—religiously, you might say—on a game or a match. Do we wish to send a message that we approve of this?"

Kennedy had never seen Townsend demonstrate any particular conviction, but he liked the tenor of this idea, having seen many lives ruined by gambling. He also knew the king loved to make laws, and if he could hide behind the defense of the realm he'd be happy to do so. In some ways, this reminded him of the days when he'd advised James, then only a boy, that he could strengthen his command by dividing and conquering as the Romans had, and that this should be his strategy against the powerful nobles threatening his reign.

One afternoon, James had returned from a hunt and set his quiver of arrows on the table. Kennedy picked it up and pitched it into his lap.

"Here," he said softly. "Break this quiver in half."

The boy, only fifteen, just stared at him, knowing it was impossible.

"Can't you do it?" Kennedy was almost whispering.

Obediently, James rose, gripped the quiver and tried to maneuver it into a position that gave his youthful strength some purchase, but the slipperiness of the many ash rods and the shiny leather of the quiver itself made this an awkward embarrassment.

"Nae, I canna do it," he finally admitted, "not with just my hands, or even over my knee."

"But you can, lad. Let a frail old man show you how." And with that, Kennedy slyly extracted one arrow at a time, snapping each easily, until they were so many splinters on the floor.

James sat there amazed, understanding completely, and in the early years of his reign he was to break the Livingstons and the Douglases one at a time in similar fashion, ultimately knifing William, the eighth earl of Douglas, at the Black Dinner in Stirling in February 1452. Indeed, the lesson of the quiver was one he'd learned all too well.

Now, studying Townsend, Kennedy considered that with

this king the laws themselves didn't matter as much as their political significance. "The last vote was close, was it not?"

"Aye, your grace, two changed votes could swing it."

"And what of those two votes? Can they be had?" Kennedy asked with a wry grin, already knowing the answer and impressed with Townsend's ingenuity.

Townsend beamed at him. "Ah, well, unless others have changed their stance, which I doubt, there are two votes converted to the ban."

"And those would be?"

"They would be the Red Douglas and—well, your grace, myself."

Kennedy then pressed him for as much detail as possible, and Townsend, having bet on virtually every major golf and football match, was able to provide an abundance of evidence. And even though Kennedy suspected he spoke more as a participant than a parliamentarian, within an hour or so his scribes had taken down his argument for James. "This has excellent potential," he concluded. "The king will like it. I'll speak with him on the morrow."

"But the biggest golf match of the year is this Sunday, your grace," Townsend blustered. "It's the perfect time to make a strong statement of the royal will. It should be canceled before the contest, you know, for the greatest effect."

"That's a good point, Ruadri. Perhaps he might see me today. As a matter of fact, you should accompany me, in the event he requires additional details. He's here, as you know, and in this weather not likely to be out hunting or fishing."

Townsend was delighted, not having had many opportunities to rub shoulders with his king.

Kennedy immediately sent a page to James's office, and

within fifteen minutes he returned, breathless, to report that the bishop should present himself to the king's secretary as soon as possible. So he and Townsend headed across the courtyard at once through the rain and wind, arriving both disheveled and optimistic, Townsend because his hopes were about to be realized, and Kennedy because there was a good body of evidence to support an edict that would benefit a great many throughout society.

Within ten minutes, the secretary informed them that James would hear their argument within the hour in the great hall.

AGAIN, Kennedy and Townsend made their way outside, across the courtyard to the East Range and the great hall. James had taken the inside route through the kitchen and surprised everyone by emerging through one of the servants' doors, carrying a shank of lamb wrapped in a linen napkin in his left hand. During the usual bows and niceties, Townsend beamed and Kennedy smiled. Guards were at attention and the scribes were poised to record the conversation.

"So," James nearly shouted, his voice echoing through the hall, "you claim the time is right to make the longbows ready! Ban golf and football, eh?"

Kennedy and Townsend exchanged nervous glances.

"Because it'll provide time to practice archery in our national defense," the king continued, then fell silent and walked about as if debating what to say next, before rounding on his visitors. "Details!" he shouted. "Explain how we present it to Parliament so they'll embrace it without a fight."

Kennedy, having eyed the king throughout his animated entry and opening comments, marched flawlessly through the case, presenting details and adding interpretations that left Townsend surprised and impressed.

James recalled how frequently the English had cut down the Scottish infantry with a hail of death from their longbows and wondered why his father had never convinced the Scots to master the bow themselves—an element of warfare they'd never completely embraced, retaining the shiltron—an assembly of men, long spears and shields—as their primary strategy. Maybe, then, the people needed to be shocked into improving not just archery but all martial arts; and this, of course, would make James a military leader.

On the other side of the great hall, he spun on one heel and waved the partially eaten shank, his long robe spiraling after him. "This is *right*! My father never pushed enough for this, but we'll change the military minds at last. And I'll fulfill my father's wish."

Townsend noticed the brief smile that crossed Kennedy's features as James continued to pace, suggesting how the parliamentarians should be approached, offering favors to some and taking them back from others, Petair Sutherland among them.

Townsend finally stepped forward. "Excuse me, your majesty," he said. " 'Tis not a battle. The measure failed last year by only three votes. It's not likely there will be many changes of heart, but there are two."

James strode slowly but deliberately toward him, stopping face-to-face.

"Two votes, then, will swing it?"

"Aye, your majesty, they will."

"And Townsend, my friend, do we know which votes those might be?"

"Aye, your majesty, we do."

"Whose?"

Townsend couldn't repress a small quivering grin. "Well, your majesty, the Red Douglas has told me personally that he has changed his stance."

"That is one, but the other? Whose might be the other?"

"Mine, your majesty," Townsend croaked.

James stared without expression into the pallid, perspiring face before him and then draped an arm—the shank still dangling from his hand—over Townsend's shoulder.

"Then it's done, eh?" he said, smiling broadly.

He instructed Kennedy on the drafting of the document, but his voice trailed off and he turned back to Townsend. "One more question," he whispered. "How will we ever find out if that shepherd lad from Boarhills can take MacGregor?"

Townsend blinked hard, his eyes bulging, and Kennedy glanced at the floor and then back up at James and Townsend.

"Well?" James said, grinning wildly. "Which would it have been, Townsend?"

"Ah, your majesty—I mean, was I a betting man, my money would be on MacGregor, my lord."

"And are you not a betting man, Townsend?" He smiled at the noble's obvious discomfort.

"Well, I've only wagered a groat or two in my day, your majesty," he lied, "but this issue is far too important to Scotland for people to be idly wagering on the outcome of some game. Which is why I raise it."

"That's well said, very well said, Ruadri," James said, then dabbed at his lips with his napkin. Townsend was thrilled to hear the king address him personally. He turned to the two of them. "This is right. The people are out of control, and they must be brought into line. Furthermore, *now* is the time—*before* the match. It'll be my statement. And don't forget the footballers; they're a rowdy bunch anyway, and they should fight the English the way they fight each other. Take it to session in the morning, Townsend," James concluded. "Take Kennedy to support you, or, better yet, have him introduce it as my emissary. All will know I'll sign it into law at their vote. But Townsend, are you positive Douglas will come over?"

"Aye, your majesty. He told me on his sacred honor. We made a deal."

"Sacred honor? The man has no honor of any kind. But be that as it may, it is done."

His petitioners turned to leave, now with their marching orders. But James caught Townsend's shoulder with his free hand and pulled him aside. "Patersone could take MacGregor," he said under his breath. "You could bet the whole lot on it, eh?" And with that, he broke into a grand royal guffaw and slapped him on the back.

Townsend, though unnerved, could only grin, since his royal majesty had, after all, just done him the favor of his life.

Townsend and Kennedy were transported in the royal carriage to Perth that very evening, and so it was, on the next day, Friday, March 4, 1457, that the edict was voted into law. It immediately had to be copied many times over so that all sheriffs and burgh commissioners could obtain one from the register clerk and then proclaim it throughout the towns and counties of the realm. The edict would be announced at St. Andrews on Sunday, March 6, at morning mass, which most everyone would be attending before the final match.

. . .

Though Morgunn was back on the farm, Olandra and Eta were still together in Cupar, helping with chores and enjoying the comforts of family. The story of the raid had been relived in detail numerous times, each one a cleansing, but they never revealed the sordid details of their agreement or the ferocity of Micael's defense.

On Thursday, March 3, a young man with a dog appeared at the house, looking furtively over his shoulder as if fearing someone had followed him. He delivered a letter to Olandra and Eta in which Morgunn wished them well, told them he was fine, and explained that the strangest accident had occurred early on Tuesday: Domni's office had burned to the ground and the lender himself was killed.

> A grisly scene, but absolutely nothing was left, nor had any documents been filed. Then the flesher came to the farm the next day and took two of the animals. It was a blessing, and after we sat talking at the table for a while it was clear that Mordiac had been lying to us both. Now the future looks bright, though perhaps it's not yet safe to return home, not until we see what this strange news might bring. No one has caught so much as a glimpse of Townsend.

He concluded by saying that Micael had told him Caeril was well and his wound healing.

Eta and Olandra embraced for a long moment. "God has excused us, I think," Eta said. "So relieved I am, havin' made such a mess of it."

"I also, child, but there's still a few bits I'm needin' to know."

"Aye, Mother," she said forthrightly.

"Ye told me he quickened ye. Tell me now, was that yer body or yer heart?"

Embarrassed, Eta sat silently, twisting her hands in her lap and staring at the floor.

"Eta, sorry I am to ask, but I might help ye if I knew."

Her daughter's mouth opened as if to speak, but for a long moment the silence remained.

"Eta."

Her eyes turned to her mother with a confused expression of fear, sadness and hope. " 'Twas my heart, I think, Mother," she whispered.

Olandra sat down on the bench, put an arm around her shoulder and rested her other palm on Eta's twisting hands, which stopped at the touch. "Then it has happened, child."

"What?"

"It happened to me on the first day I saw yer father."

Eta turned toward her.

"I didn't really notice at first, but somethin' made me watch his every move and expression, and the longer I watched, the stronger it grew, though I had yet to speak a word to him."

"Not even hello?"

"Not a word. Then I found myself movin' to where I thought he'd go next, and then, all of a sudden, we was face-to-face." Eta was now wide-eyed and beginning to smile.

"And then?" Olandra asked.

"Dinna matter. All I knew was that this person had somehow attached himself to my heart and unless I followed through I might never be the same.

"That," Eta whispered, "is what happened to me."

"Aye, child. It must be. Seems ye should've left the match when he was doin' poorly. Your task was done then."

"I knew that, Mother, but I couldna leave. I had to watch him. But face-to-face, well . . ."

"Oh? Tell me."

Eta described the situation in the pit with Caeril talking to himself and she herself encouraging him when his back was turned.

"What did he do when ye spoke? Could he hear ye?"

"Aye, Mother, he turned round after the second time. I was right there, just a few paces away, with the others watchin' the match. I dunna think they knew."

"At times like that, child, there is no one else on earth."

"His eyes was so beautiful. He looked scared at first, but then, in an instant—when he saw it was me, I think—he went calm, then turned round and hit the ball, and everybody started yellin'. I guess it was hard to do. And when the ball rolled all the way to where Mr. Gille-Copain and Micael was, Caeril went runnin'."

"And his expression had changed when he turned?"

"Aye."

"Ah, that was it, Eta. Like yer father told me so many times, when we were face-to-face, he felt he loved me—dinna know why, but he loved me still."

"Oh, my," was all Eta could say, and several long moments passed before she finally spoke again.

"But I tried to do somethin' very wrong to him. Why would he even speak to me, ever?"

"I dunno, Eta, but I'd guess you'll find out soon enough."

The Edict

UNLIKE THE WEEK PRIOR, Sunday was cool and clear with very little wind. A great day for golf, they all thought, as they took in the sounds and sights of the mass at Holy Trinity. Bishop Kennedy's words were comforting, but not at all slanted toward his usual themes of fair play and tradition. He spoke today of temper, of dedication, of national pride. The players agonized through these overly familiar subjects, itching to stride off into the links. Caeril's thoughts drifted to the match at hand, hoping against hope to hold his game together by the patterns that he knew would result in successful shots. His hand was indeed healing well, and he would also steel himself against any other outside interference. He now knew *any* distraction need not be monumental to distract him fatally.

MacGregor, on the other hand, was sensing an unusual tone in Bishop Kennedy's message. Why was he not extolling the righteousness of fair play and honor between men? And where was Lord Sutherland? He shifted in his seat, concerned.

As the bishop concluded, and before the benediction, he instructed everyone to remain seated for the reading of a special edict that was directly relevant to all subjects from this day forward. But whereas MacGregor felt an ominous flush, Caeril was merely agitated. Others exchanged sidelong glances and some rolled their eyes at this harassment from above, but most sat there resigned for one more delay before they commenced the day's most important matter.

On the final *amen,* the parishioners shifted as Kennedy strode from the altar and stopped at the foot of the pulpit steps, where with great flair he was presented with a sealed parchment scroll. This occasioned yet more shifting.

He ascended to the pulpit and stared expressionless out over the congregants; his voice almost erupted in the silence of the nave, echoing through that great stone space. The words at first meant nothing, just another edict, but then, as the second sentence floated across the pews, *"that the Futeboll and golfe be utterly cryit downe, and not be usit,"* the devastating reality sank in: four times each year there would be a showing of weapons; targets would be erected at churches; every man between the ages of twelve and fifty would shoot at least six arrows between Easter and Halloween and those who didn't fined two pence each, such money used to buy drinks for those who did.

But what blunted their minds was that golf and football were henceforth forbidden. They all prayed that this prohibition would not begin today, when only one match remained to be played. Surely not!

Kennedy stood high above them, staring down into their disbelieving eyes. "From this day on," he concluded, "no, from this *moment* on, no golf played." And suddenly it was clear that no championship would be decided, either on this Sunday or in the foreseeable future.

They sat, immobilized, ambushed and thwarted, this news delivered by the very man who had sprung from the loins of Scottish legend, raised their kings and served as their spiritual leader. Not one man had the words to capture their shock and dismay.

With a bowed head and a grave expression, Bishop Kennedy descended the steps and went out through the priest's side door, believing he'd done his country a great service and leaving his flock in stunned silence.

There would be no march down the Scores to the bridge and the links beyond, no pronouncements or warnings by the United Golf Honours Society, no introductions or coin toss, neither crushing drives nor deft approaches, miraculous recoveries, or painfully curling hole-outs—no excitement, *no golf at all.*

They milled about in the street outside, knowing that a dark time lay ahead for their game. People would put away their clubs so as to not succumb to the urges of the flying or rolling ball. Adam would return to his forge, Nectan to his family business, Colaim to his government offices, John to his plow. Only Caeril would carry his clubs out into the links, but without the competitions even he would hit fewer and fewer balls.

Here and elsewhere, all players and followers—including Petair Sutherland, sitting in a church in Perth—quietly cursed King James's meanness. *Archers?* he thought, *He'll not be turning us to the bow, unless 'tis aimed at his heart!*

As stunned as everyone else, Caeril walked alone toward the links. So many sad days had passed for him within the familiar comfort of the dunes and fescue, the sound of water and wind and birds and sheep. He remembered how, when his father died, when he'd lost animals and dogs, when he penalized himself, the links had soothed him. He could never say how long he stayed there on this Sunday. With neither flock nor golf he just wandered about and sat finally on a high dune in the crisp air, looking out at the strangely placid surf, a light breeze rustling his hair.

He was lost in thought when he heard, seemingly from far away, a voice saying his name. For an instant he thought God was calling to him, but as the sound came nearer he recognized that it was Micael.

"Brother," his friend said, "this is a sad place."

"Aye," answered Caeril. "Sad it is."

Silence prevailed as Micael sat by him on the dune, the two of them staring out over the landscape like cats at a fire.

It was Caeril who broke the peace. "Will we ever play again, do ye think?"

"Dunno."

"Hope so."

Minutes went by, until a flock moving into the small valley before them and a shepherd's calls broke their reverie and returned their attention to the world.

"Caeril," Micael said, "I came to tell ye some things—important things."

"What could be important after Kennedy's readin'?"

"Several things."

"Such as?"

"Well, I spoke with Morgunn Ayr again," Micael said.

Caeril just turned and looked at him.

"He said no record of the agreement with Domni was found in the fire."

Caeril didn't move.

"He also said he was grateful the flesher came by to take some of his animals for slaughter. That Domni had been lyin' to them both."

Silence still.

"He told me Eta and her mother would return in a week or so."

Now Caeril turned to Micael and said, simply, "And?"

"That they was in Cupar, with family."

"Dunna care," Caeril said coldly.

"Oh?" said Micael, sounding surprised. "Well, there's somethin' else I need to tell ye."

For just an instant, Caeril wondered if he might already have seen Eta. "Tell me," he managed to say.

"I been spendin' some time near Kingsbarns."

"Why there?"

Micael's grin was somewhat pained. "Well, my uncle introduced me to a friend of his over there and his—uh, daughter."

"Uh-oh." Caeril finally smiled. "Now ye have my attention."

"Aye, afraid to tell ye, I am, but it's so good I may have to take a few steps."

"Well," said Caeril, now smiling broadly, "I think I know what steps you're referrin' to. Ye're a close rascal. Who is she?"

"Forester's daughter."

"Should've known."

"So, Caeril, what about Eta?"

"Eta's been botherin' me, sure. She tried to destroy me, eh?" he said, showing his change of heart and fixing a stare on Micael.

"Aye, she nearly did ye in. But lookin' back, she should've left when ye was reelin'."

Caeril sat, squinting into the bright sky. "Maybe she just liked seein' me down."

"She liked watchin' ye struggle more than savin' her own home? Why do ye think she dunna leave?"

"Who's to say? Why dunna ye tell me, then."

"I canna say what's in *your* head. Mine dunna matter."

They turned back toward town and saw in the distance the unmistakable white mane of Angus Gille-Copain. Their route to the bridge would take them within hailing distance, but as they drew near Angus saw them and they converged.

The edict had affected everyone, especially the players, but for Angus it was the apparent end of a lifetime of memories, his sadness so obvious that the boys were moved.

"Well, lads," Angus said, "how many times will we have to chase King Henry back to England before they raise this foolish ban? Did ye see the constables and soldiers and burghers roamin' about—even some monks? We couldna *kick* a rock into a scrape out here."

The three men looked at one another, realizing then that their game, though temporarily stopped, was as inherent to them as breathing. They also felt they had an obligation to preserve the stories they knew, which Angus told so well.

"Angus, if I may call ye thus," Caeril said, "might we gather at Tippin's tonight? They canna take that from us, can they? Maybe share a few tales?"

"Aye, I'm goin'. I *was* goin' there anyway, ye know, to carve the bar. I've got your face pretty good here in my pocket. Now I'll just have to save it."

Caeril knew this was the ultimate compliment, and he reveled in the thought of his image there in solid oak beside his idols. Then reality swept in with another rush of remorse as he watched Angus walk slowly over the Swilcan Bridge.

Micael shook his head and said, "It's hours till sundown, so let me show ye the collection of bows at my father's stand up on Merkagait Street. At least they'll be doin' a boomin' business today."

But the sun does not linger in the late-winter sky, and before long a number of players and their friends were pushing through the door at Tippin's, tonight a somber place.

Samsone MacLeod and Baithin Douglas were already on their way home, having long journeys ahead of them, but Nectan MacGregor, Adam Paternis and Colaim Cummings were sitting at the bar. John Brighte and Mal-Giric Alexander would have been in some tavern regardless, so they too were present. While Micael didn't regularly attend these affairs, several of them smiled as he came inside with Caeril.

The group, if smaller than the usual championship crowd, was still an eruption in process. The many intense and raucous times spent in Eldon Tippin's establishment in past years had created an exclusive atmosphere, and they all felt safe here among friends. The entire day they'd been in a stupor, reluctant to express their disappointment in public, but within these walls they railed against the ban, shouting down the misguidedness of government in general and Parliament in particular. Before long, the tirade had expanded to include King James; Brighte led the charge, fueled by malt and mead, with the younger players and clubmen following suit, all of them howling up a mortal din.

Eldon eyed them without concern because these men never moved on from brutal language to hooliganism. Instead, their tirades evolved into a contest, with one after the next taking the stage to deliver some banal or, in a few cases, surprisingly eloquent expression of their frustration. Every vicious, discrediting remark would be met with equally boisterous confirmations, one after the other, until it all dissolved, finally, into laughter. What else could they do?

Brighte stepped forward, clearly hitting his stride, and waved his mug aloft. "So I ask ye, lads, how long can they keep us down? How does this ban differ from bein' cut off by your woman, eh? It ain't natural, right?"

"Nae, nae!" the chorus shouted.

"Canna be long, lads, afore we'll be back! Sure, we can play their games with the longbow, but we'll be back to what we like; to what made us," he shouted triumphantly. His audience roared in angry agreement.

At the mention of the fair sex, Gille-Copain fell silent, but no one noticed except Colaim Cummings, as the two were sitting together at a small corner table.

"Angus," Colaim whispered, "this business sits poorly with you, eh?"

Angus simply shook his head and turned to watch the proceedings.

Colaim, concerned about his dour mood, felt compelled to encourage him to talk. "So tell me, please."

Angus glanced at him and then inspected the tabletop, gently nodding his head. "Aye, it is a blow, this, that somehow brings back many ill thoughts."

"About our game?" Colaim asked.

"Nae, nae, other things."

"True enough," Colaim said. "In times of great disappointment, other thoughts can manifest themselves. But it's also true you're a strong enough man to hold firm against them."

"That's good of ye, but sadness tends to multiply, dunnit?" Angus said, then turned tables on Colaim. "I wasn't thinkin' it would ever come up, but what of yer last hole against Nectan? Ye seemed troubled on that last roll for the half."

"Could you tell?" Colaim answered, somewhat surprised, and suspecting Angus might be merely changing the subject.

"Aye, ye winced, like ye was hurt, but I couldna tell where it might of happened."

"Nae, not that day, since you ask. It's been coming on for a while. To be honest, sometimes it's troublesome just to walk."

"Well, none of us is gettin' any younger, now, are we? But I'm old enough to be yer father. It's just somethin' passin'."

"I hope so, but it seems worse. My father, you know—well, he's long gone now, but there's times like this I miss him still. My wife's a comfort, though. Mary knows about my legs."

This returned Angus to his silent stupor, and for the first time Colaim realized that grief was seated deep within him, perhaps something involving those he loved the most.

By now, the shouting had subsided and the low hum of conversation filled the room. Micael was sitting nearby, talking with two of the younger players; Alphonso MacPhee, Nectan's clubman, and Caeril soon joined them. Micael could hear what Colaim and Angus were saying behind him, even as he followed the conversation at his own table.

Angus was quietly explaining his many blessings. "I was comfortable enough with meself, liked in my work, and I loved the links and knew in due time I'd have a family."

"I understand you do have a fine family. Will not your son succeed you?"

"Aye, he will," he said with a brief smile.

"Angus," Colaim told him, "sure, we're all unhappy with

the ban, but you seem to have some deeper trouble. It might help to tell a friend."

They sat in silence for a moment or two, the younger man patiently and the other wrestling with his thoughts. "Colaim," he said, "my life seems always to have been about the second time around. A worthless spearman I was and vowed if I ever had the chance, I'd do better."

"And you did, as I understand."

"Aye, 'twas good fortune, that."

"Nonetheless."

"And the game—well, I thought maybe I could make it to the finals even before ye were born, Colaim."

"It's fickle business."

"Fickle? Aye, a good term."

"Tell me about your game, then," Colaim said.

"Far—aye, I could hit it far—and a good roller I was, but around the fair greens, in competition, time after time I failed to convert more often than not. I never won anything but the most menial matches."

Colaim placed a hand on his shoulder. "But did you love the game?"

"Maybe too much. As a player, my mind wasn't sturdy to the task. Ye and yer friends, Colaim—ah, so many times I've been amazed. I could only dream that my comical little fluffs and skulls over the fair greens could've been magic, but nae. One or two here and there, maybe, but never enough. So"—he sighed—"my second choice was findin' holes—and I was lucky at that. As a player I knew what to do and couldna've, but the findin' seemed so natural. I liked to make each one a little story or a song, where ye or Adam or Nectan could do magical things. It was, I suppose, my fulfillment, this second chance. Glad I am it came my way—though now I'm afraid it's gone."

"Not gone, just stopped. Our game will outlast Parliament and even kings," Colaim said, grinning. "Gille-Copain, you have no equal. *A little story.* That sets you apart from the rest. And after all these years, now it comes to me. Every hole's a little tale that tells itself to everyone. It's not just a stretch of grass and dunes and pits, aye, bonny as they may be, it's the *story.* God bless you, my friend, you've made us all better—and, I may add, your encouragement has meant more to me than you could ever know."

Angus looked him in the eye. "At times it seemed the parts of many holes, the little wrinkles and dips, were only for me—that I was the only one who knew them. And this felt—well, frivolous, I suppose."

"Oh, nae, my friend. I'd wager that if you called us all together, we could name them, each and every one."

They stared at each other, still smiling, one in gratefulness, the other in appreciation.

"Thank ye," Angus said, "though it's gone."

"Nae possible," Colaim stated matter-of-factly. "And we dare not let anyone forget."

"Aye," Angus said. "Caeril and Micael said something of the sort earlier, to meet when we can and make sure not to forget."

These two, hearing their names, turned from their table toward Gille-Copain and Cummings.

Colaim acknowledged them and said, "We owe it to ourselves, lads, and to the game, to keep it alive in our stories, and I suggest that Angus here should enlarge our store of them this very evening, in spite *or because* of everything else that's happened." Then, sensing that Angus was on the verge of declining, he added, "And there might be another story as yet untold, since Adam has mentioned a lovely lass in his match with Caeril."

Caeril turned a dark shade of red and Micael broke a smile.

"A loss of composure there, eh, lad?" Colaim asked. "There must be more to that story. She could have knocked you over with a feather, the way you played for a while."

Everyone laughed save for Caeril, who was too embarrassed to do anything but grin and blush, and Angus, who was staring down at the table. But then he raised his eyes to Caeril, as he was sitting quite close, and said quietly, "Might that have been the start of somethin' or the end?"

"Uh, I really dunno," Caeril mumbled feebly.

Angus eyed him. "Which is it, then?"

Colaim watched, fascinated by Angus's directness as he stared at Caeril like a father upon an erring son.

"Caeril," he said softly, "if there *is* somethin'—look at me, lad—then it's dangerous ground and ye must be sure which it is, beginnin' or end. Dunna leave an empty hole in your life." With that, Angus rose to his feet, walked to the bar and asked Eldon for another splash of single malt. They all watched him raise his mug to his lips, closed one eye and drink it off. Then he placed the mug quietly on the bar, and when Eldon held up the bottle as if to offer a refill he gently pushed his mug forward. Once filled, there it sat, as did Angus, with his head bowed.

Awkwardly, the conversation continued on other subjects, with most not knowing for sure what had just transpired.

Colaim then walked to Angus's side and again placed a hand on his shoulder.

"My friend, that came from the depths."

"Aye, but I shouldna've said it. The lad's probably all a-scramble as it is, without old men tellin' him how to live his life."

"Don't burden yourself with that, Angus. He's young, he'll sort it out."

"Nae, Colaim. Once I was young too, and I dinna sort it out, not at all. I found her, Colaim, and I've never told any-body. I was young—and scared of her sayin' nae or whatever. Missed my chance, I did. Thought there would be others. Lucky for me there finally was, but that first one was the perfection that I lost"—he paused—"and I've never been able to clear it away. Aye. I've a family—happy, proud even, but what might it have been had I the courage? There's a hole there, and it's with me still."

"Ah, so that's it, then," said Colaim.

Angus's steady concentration on his pewter mug was confirmation enough, so Colaim patted his shoulder lightly, turned and walked back to Caeril and Micael.

"Lads, it's not likely Angus'll be telling us stories tonight. He's feeling poorly, and we should all go home anyway. It's late, and tomorrow's another day of work, is it not? I have to go back to Perth myself on precious little sleep. Let's all say good night, then, and especially to Angus." This last bit he announced to the room, and one by one they all went up to wish Angus well.

Caeril waited until last, watching as Angus lingered along the bar, running his fingers over each carved image. Then Angus shook Eldon's hand and started for the door, where he sensed Caeril's presence and stopped.

"I had no right to speak to ye thus," he said, "Caeril, I'm sorry. This business has brought out the worst in me."

Caeril, fumbling with his hat, was completely at a loss. "I—uh, wanted to wish ye well."

Angus, also embarrassed, simply nodded his head, shook Caeril's hand and toed the thresh on the floor.

"And to thank ye, sir," Caeril said.

Another nod.

"Can I come down to see ye from time to time?"

"Anytime, sure; I have a place ye can stay. Please do."

Then they walked out the door, Angus heading for his lodgings in town.

Caeril watched him go and turned in the other direction, toward Boarhills—back to his life. But after a hundred yards he stopped and suddenly spun around as though uncertain of his destination. Up the street, he could see Micael waiting for him, dimly lit by a candle in a nearby window.

They came face-to-face with enough light for each to see the other's expression: Micael's curious and Caeril's quietly confident. "Will ye tell me, then," Caeril said, "how to go about findin' Eta over in Cupar?"

AFTER

THE GAME WAS RELEGATED to secrecy and the links were returned to the shepherds—still allowed to play, but only alone—and the archers, the fishermen repairing nets, and the others: cutting sod, drying clothes, hunting and walking. They ground their way through the seasons, sorely missing the excitement of competition and the fellowship of play.

But the ban did not last as long as anyone feared. More important things filled the minds of the Old Lords. On August 3, 1460, on a stormy day well south of the Firth of Forth, James II was leading an assault on Roxburgh, a decidedly strategic castle held by the English army of Henry VI. The actual Queen's Cannons were in tow, and James was about to show Henry that Scotland was a force with which to be reckoned. Just as the attack was about to be joined, James—wishing to see his wife's dowry in action—approached a cannon crew preparing for the bombardment. The troops, including a new contingent of Scottish archers, stood poised to bring the wrath of Scotland down upon the invaders and drive them out of their country once and for all.

"Show me the glory of its power!" James commanded, and the cannoneer flashed the touch hole. Unfortunately, the cannonball barely made it out of the muzzle. The stern of the weapon failed metallurgically, blasting cast-iron shrapnel of colossal size and weight to the rear and taking out a squad of men along with their king.

James's death was a significant loss, of course, though the troops surged forward and took the castle, indeed sending Henry's army on its way south.

Kennedy, as the senior Old Lord, was again given the task of protecting and educating nine-year-old James III, just as he had raised his late father, and along with the boy's mother, Queen Mary, and the other Old Lords, he was soon consumed with organizing the affairs of state. They had neither time nor patience for continuing the suppression of sport, and scarcely before the dust and smoke from that mortal blast had settled, players were back on the links. People played both golf and football freely as before for thirteen more years, until another edict banned them again—but that was short-lived, as was the last attempt in 1491. Finally, the advent of small arms and gunpowder obviated the longbow forever and, with it, golf's threat to national security. The game and the people's right to play it would never again be challenged.

In time, John Knox and religious fundamentalism ravaged the nation in the name of God, so desecrating the cathedral, the castle and the priory that they eventually became quarries for constructing new buildings in town and enlarging the harbor pier—an epic travesty against architecture and history. The ecclesiastic and educational center of the Scottish universe drifted away from St. Andrews like clouds and the Auld

Grey Toon slid sadly, like an old drunk, into the doldrums of anonymity.

And then golf pulled this city—named for one of the twelve blessed disciples, the patron saint of the land—back into the limelight. No longer a spiritual and intellectual epicenter, St. Andrews reemerged as the world symbol of golf, Scotland's own natural game.

In 1503, a major breakthrough for both golf and the Scots occurred when James IV, that glittering but tragic king, married Margaret Tudor, daughter of Henry VII of England, thus freeing his nation from the need to defend itself and allowing its citizens to relax somewhat. It is recorded that on September 21, 1502, James spent the colossal sum of fourteen shillings on clubs from the bower at St. Johnston, and five months later he must have been hooked because this time he spent forty-two shillings for more balls and clubs getting ready for a match with the Earle of Bothuile.

It is likely that during this time the game became popular with the wealthy. Nobility always led the way, and with the inference of the bans still ringing in their ears, the wealthy played and the gentry watched. The people must have been somewhat happier being at least able to watch the game. It was better than no golf at all and a likely source of wild hilarity in the taverns. In fact, this situation may have formed the social structure of the game as we know it today.

But while golf seems to survive anything, politics continued to be fickle. The Treaty of Perpetual Amity between these two countries lasted all of fifteen years, sundered by greed and stupidity. James himself, along with a significant group of nobles later called the Flower of Scottish Nobility, was killed at Flodden in 1513 in a needless battle.

Succeeding at the age of one was James V, who, upon

maturity, would have been very popular with twenty-first-century paparazzi; eventually, his daughter became the legendary Mary, Queen of Scots, who with her chosen mate, Lord Darnley, brought forth James VI and some long overdue sanity.

The historic charter of St. Andrews was proclaimed in 1552 by Archbishop John Hamilton and the town council, which decreed that its citizens had *the right to this public ground, for golf, fute-boll, shuting, and all games.* They had won. And we, the world, had won. The triumphal return to brilliance of the city of St. Andrews had begun.

James VI reputedly had a very severe golf bug as well. Shortly after his ascension to the Scottish *and* English thrones in 1603, he declared that golf could be played everywhere, the only stipulation being that it could not be played on Sunday until after church (it was this King James who authorized the 1611 English version of the Bible that is still in use). His grandfather had introduced the game to the whole of Britain, but the grandson made it commercial and, true to form, appointed a Royal Clubmaker in 1603. Golf never wavered after James VI. Fifteen years later he created an official ball-making operation and set a ceiling price of four shillings per ball because the Dutch were demanding exorbitant prices for the balls they made. James VI was, after all, a Scot.

In affixing names to golf's origins, the Stewart King Jameses, II, IV and VI, should not go unmentioned. John Hamilton would also have to be remembered, as would Hugh Lyon Playfair, the ruthless but dedicated provost mayor of St. Andrews. But never, ever take primary credit away from the countless common shepherds who played on through wind, rain and political tempest. If you really wanted to be a snob, you could throw in the names of Caeril Patersone and Micael Carrick.

In the darkness of the ban, archery was reborn and contests blossomed more to satisfy the Scots' competitive needs than to hone their military skill. But it did not take them long to learn that their matches would be played for second place. For nearly twenty years, no one ever unseated Micael Carrick, whose trusty attendant was Caeril Patersone. The talk of Scotland, Micael led all competitors at Peebles, Selkirk and Stirling, trimmed all the boys at St. Andrews University and won at Kilwinning and Edinburgh. When golf resumed, he and Caeril took dual prizes in their respective sports at Musselburgh many years running. They were the most celebrated pair in the country, befriended by royalty and the officials of every burgh.

You can find many other details in the marvelous archives of the University of St. Andrews and the St. Andrews Golf Museum.

Adam Paternis was for many years regarded the symbol of golf—long after his game deserted him. Colaim Cummings was not even able to walk, late in his life. Nectan MacGregor developed hip problems and then some back ailments that prevented him from playing his delayed championship with Patersone. However, he continued on as a revered figure in the game, succeeding Angus Gille-Copain as the hole finder following Angus's death in the fall of the year that Caeril won his sixth title. From that day forward, partly because Nectan was somewhat hobbled but mostly in reverence to Angus, they placed a flag in each hole to stand by itself—as if his smiling ghost were there to encourage them on—and there they stand to this day.

Eta and Caeril, a love affair for the ages, brought forth two sons, the elder winning the championship twice, the other developing new clubs and balls. In addition, there were three fabulously beautiful daughters, tintypes of their mother, the first moving off to Musselburgh to marry into the Park family, whereas the other two stayed closer to home, in St. Andrews, one marrying Albus Robertson and her sister young T. William Morris, all three in the year 1481. In this way, seeds were sown that would blossom in those three families hundreds of years later, to thrill the crowds and change the world of golf.

But Eta and Caeril? She was his heroine, and he was her life.

Of all the items listed in the masterful Declaration of Arbroath, the statement of Scottish independence drawn up in 1320, after freedom, glory, riches and honor, there was one that is perhaps left unspoken: golf. Freedom was everything. Scots would cease their battles on the links when they needed to fight wars to preserve it, but otherwise the game was primary. Golf was second fiddle only to freedom.

The 1457 edict reads like this in Middle Scots:

> It is decretit and ordanit, that the wapinschawing be halden by the Lordis and the Barronis spirituall and temporall, foure tymis in the zeir. And that the futball and golfe be utterly cryit downe, and not be usit, and that the bow markis be made, at ilk paroche kirk a pair of buttis. And schuting be usit ilk sonday. And that ilk man schute 6 schottis at the leist, under the pane to be rasit spone thame, that cummis not at the leist 2 p to be gevin to thame that cummis to the bow markis to drink. And this is to be usit fra Pasche till Alhollowmes efter. And be the nixt midsomer to be reddy withal thair graith without failzie. And that thair be a bowar and a flegear in ilk heid towne of the Schire. And that the towne furnies him of stuf and graith, efter as nedis him thairto, that thay may serve the cuntrie with. And as tuiching the fute-ball and the golfe to be punist be the Baronis unlaw, and gif he takis not the unlaw, that it be takin be the kings officiaris. And gift the parochin be mekill, that thair be three or foure or fyve bow markis and past 12 zeiris sall use schuting.

ACKNOWLEDGMENTS

Having now seen something of the inner workings of the publishing industry, I realize there are doubtless many people whom I should thank but whose names I have never learned. The cleansing of a manuscript is a thing to behold; hearing talk of restrictive or non-restrictive words delivered with the calmness of surgeons scrubbing up by the operating room. It was comforting but somewhat demoralizing knowing that my untouched words laid bare would have been something less than their professional standard.

But I do know one Gary Fisketjon at Knopf, and I would thank all of those unseen souls by thanking him. His talent for readability is amazing. He has changed the way I will look at assembled words from now on. And, perhaps it was chance, but Gary is, as we say in my business, a stick. He can golf his ball, and in that we became brothers chasing a story with the same fire. Thank you, Gary. May you never ever take more than two putts on any green.

I would also like to thank Dr. W. W. Knox, chairman of the History Department at the University of St. Andrews, for his thorough review, comments and advice. Bill is the coauthor of the consummate compilation of Scottish history to date as well as numerous other books and articles, and possesses a spectacular *curriculum vitae.*

Thanks are also due to Alan J. R. MacGregor, the general manager of the St. Andrews golf operation, who assisted me with connections to facts and details that made the book that much more accurate and, for me anyway, enjoyable.

Peter Lewis, director and curator at the St. Andrews Golf Museum, was also very helpful.

A student at the University of St. Andrews, Jessica Lockwood, researched the actual edict in the university's library early in my process. Jessica is the daughter of Steve Lockwood, who has had a positive effect on my design career through a project in Naples, Florida.

Chuck Ruttan, Esq., an original partner at Pumpkin Ridge, has not only been a great friend for fifteen years, but, through his relentless networking, eventually landed my manuscript in the hands of Gary Fisketjon.

A number of friends who read early versions of the book encouraged me to move forward. One is a fellow member of the American Society of Golf Course Architects, Doug Carrick in Toronto; others are Steve Timm, my longtime associate in Los Angeles, and Mark Goldman at home in Atlanta, where for many years now we have shared the occasional carpool to school, as well as golf games, illness, parenting and holiday meals on a regular basis.

A trio of professionals in the development industry should also be credited with assisting me in the refinement of the story. David Norden and Walter Frame, both prominent management executives for Spruce Peak at Stowe Mountain in Vermont, and their visionary guru, my great friend of twenty-five years and senior guy for many of my golf projects from coast to coast, Andy Norris. All three of them encouraged me and gave me comfort that I was not wasting their time, or mine.

I would be remiss in not thanking Jack Nicklaus, certainly for his gracious Foreword, but more for shaping my life. It is easy to see him as the greatest champion, but for those of us who have been lucky enough to be around him, the words that come immediately to mind are *loyal* and *friend*.

But at the heart of it all is my wife, Pam, who never minces words and reads everything. She doesn't just read a few novels a week, she reads the newspaper, magazines, blogs, instruction books, software agreements and the cereal box. She even reads the information that accompanies medical prescriptions, the kids' homework assignments and their textbooks, the back of her driver's license and the tags on electrical cords and pillows. Several years ago when I was first assembling ideas, she would say, "I can't read this," and so I would go back to the drawing board. It was Pam who stood over the forge as the story rolled along, hammering here and there, sometimes pretty hard, until it became a comprehensible item. Only then was I comfortable sending it off to anyone else. Thank you, Pam. We've been married twenty years, and it hasn't been long enough.

—B
Christmas, 2006

BIBLIOGRAPHY

Balfour, James. *Reminiscences of Golf on St. Andrews Links.* Edinburgh: David Douglas, 1887; reprint, Chelsea, Mich.: Ailsa, 1987.

Barclay, Gordon. *Farmers, Temples, and Tombs.* Edinburgh: Canongate Books, 1998.

Bauer, Aleck. *Hazards.* Chicago: 1931; reprint, Worcestershire: Grant Books, 1993.

Behrend, John, and Peter N. Lewis. *Challenges and Champions.* St. Andrews: Royal & Ancient Golf Club of St. Andrews, 1998, p. 473.

Best, Nicholas. *The Kings and Queens of Scotland.* London: Weidenfeld & Nicholson, 1999.

Browning, Robert. *A History of Golf.* London: J. M. Dent & Sons, 1955; reprint, Chelsea, Mich.: Ailsa, 1996.

Campbell, Ewan. *Saints and Sea Kings.* Edinburgh: Canongate Books, 1998.

Cunliffe, Barry. *The Extraordinary Voyage of Pytheas the Greek.* New York: Walker & Co., 2002.

Darwin, Bernard. *The Golf Courses of the British Isles.* London: Duckworth & Co., 1910; reprint, Storey Communications & Ailsa, 1988.

"Discovering Old St. Andrews." St. Andrews Society of St. Andrews, 1995.

Driscoll, Stephen. *Alba.* Edinburgh: Birlinn, 2002.

Dunkling, Leslie Alan. *Scottish Christian Names.* Stirling, Scotland: Johnston & Bacon, 1978–1995.

Findley, Rowe. "Scotland: Ghosts and Glory," *National Geographic,* vol. 166, no. 1 (July 1984).

Finlayson, Bill. *Wild Harvesters.* Edinburgh: Canongate Books, 1998.

Hamilton, David. *Golf, Scotland's Game.* Kilmacolm, Scotland: Patrick Press, 1998.

Harris, Nathaniel. *Heritage of Scotland.* New York: Octopus Publishing Group, 2000.

Hingley, Richard. *Settlement and Sacrifice.* Edinburgh: Canongate Books, 1998.

Houston, R. A., and W.W.J. Knox. *History of Scotland.* London: Penguin Books, 2001.

Joy, David. *The Scrapbook of Old Tom Morris.* Chelsea, Mich.: Sleeping Bear Press, 2001.

Keay, John, and Julia Keay. *Collins Encyclopedia of Scotland.* London: HarperCollinsPublishers, 1994.

Kuntz, Bob. *Antique Golf Clubs.* Ralph Maltby Enterprises, 1990.

Lamont-Brown, Raymond. *Scottish Folklore.* Edinburgh: Berlinn, 1996.

Macdonald, Charles Blair. *Scotland's Gift, Golf.* London & New York: Charles Scribner's Sons, 1928; reprint, Chelsea, Mich.: Sleeping Bear, 1985.

MacGregor, Geddes. *Scotland: An Intimate Portrait.* Boston: Houghton Mifflin Company, 1980.

Macintyre, Lorn. *St. Andrews, the Royal Burgh.* Great Britain: Pitkin, Unichrome, 2000.

MacKenzie, Alister. *The Spirit of St. Andrews.* Chelsea, Mich. : Sleeping Bear, 1995.

MacKie, J. D. *A History of Scotland.* London: Penguin Books, 1978.

Maclean, Fitzroy. *Highlanders.* New York: Viking Studio, 1995.

———. *Scotland,* rev. ed. London: Thames & Hudson, 2000.

MacLeish, Kenneth. "The Highlands of Scotland," *National Geographic,* vol. 133, no. 3 (March 1968).

Mathison, Thomas. *The Goff.* Edinburgh: 1743; reprint, Far Hills, N.J.: U.S. Golf Association, 1981.

Maxwell, Gordon. *A Gathering of Eagles.* Edinburgh: Canongate Books, 1998.

Pearson, John M. *A Guided Walk Round St. Andrews,* 3d rev. ed. Leven, Fife: Levenmouth, 1996.

Owen, Olwyn. *The Sea Road.* Edinburgh : Canongate Books, 1998.

Powike, Sir Maurice. *The Thirteenth Century,* rev. ed. Oxford: Oxford University Press, 1998.

Price, Robert. *Scotland's Golf Courses.* Aberdeen: Aberdeen University Press, 1989.

Robertson, James K. *St. Andrews, Home of Golf.* Cupar, Scotland: Innes, 1974.

Rothero, Christopher. *Scottish and Welsh Wars.* Oxford: Osprey Publishing, 1984.

Scottish National Archives. *The Queen and the Scots.* Edinburgh: Publications and Education Branch, 1998.

———. *Scottish Independence.* Edinburgh: Publications and Education Branch, 1996.

Secretary of State for Scotland. *St. Andrews Cathedral and Castle.* Hatfield, Doncaster: Besacarr Prints, 1996.

Simpson, W. G. *The Art of Golf.* Edinburgh: David Douglas, 1912; reprint, New York: Ailsa, 1992.

Smart, Veronica. *The Coins of St. Andrews.* St. Andrews: St. Andrews University Library, 1991.

Sweeny, Del. *Agriculture in the Middle Ages.* Philadelphia: University of Pennsylvania Press, 1995.

Tabraham, Christopher. *Picts.* London: Historic Scotland, 1989.

———. *St. Andrews Castle.* Edinburgh: Howie & Seath, 2001.

Tulloch, W. W. *The Life of Tom Morris.* London: T. Werner Laurie, 1908; reprint, Far Hills, N.J.: U.S. Golf Association, 1992.

U.K. Ordnance Survey. *St. Andrews & East Fife @ 1:2,500M.* Southampton, U.K.: 2003.

Wormald, Jenny. *Mary, Queen of Scots.* London: Collins & Brown, 1991.